BRONTEZ PURNELL

JOHNNY WOULD YOU LOVE ME IF MY DICK WERE BIGGER

T0161081

FEMINIST PRESS

AT THE CITY UNIVERSITY OF NEW YORK

NEW YORK CITY

Published in 2017 by the Feminist Press
at the City University of New York
The Graduate Center
365 Fifth Avenue, Suite 5406
New York, NY 10016

feministpress.org

First Feminist Press edition 2017

Second printing September 2020

Cover and text design by Drew Stevens

Library of Congress Cataloging-in-Publication Data is available for this title.

JOHNNY
WOULD YOU
LOVE ME
IF MY
DICK WERE
BIGGER

JOHNNY WOULD YOU LOVE ME
IF MY DICK WERE BIGGER
B/W
SEX WITH JUNKIES

I was an American Waiter bored at work. I had been suffering from an acute depression for two and a half years. I woke up from a two-hour nap and was about to miss my 12:05 a.m. BART train to the city. I never slept because I knew I was meant to be tired. I woke up feeling like God had punched me. I put on facial moisturizer and left the house without jerking off. I had worked for way too long at the diner and was privy to some pretty tawdry bullshit.

In that movie *Milk* I had seen how SF was once a bunch of dudes with beards (or mustaches) and flannel. Clone core. I hate nostalgia. This was not a blip on the cultural screen; this bullshit was still happening. Daily. Every night before my shift I light a prayer candle, sprinkle goat's blood over my altar, and say my chant: "I will fuck, kill, and eat all you Castro debutante bitches."

All night they play the same shit on the jukebox, and after years of repeated listening I finally allow myself to say it in my head: *I fucking hate the Smiths*. Every time I hear them all I picture is Morrissey alone in a room crying and jerking off simultaneously.

Sometimes I don't know if I feel like I don't fit in because that's what's actually happening, or if I've been a punk so long that I really don't know how to fit in, or if it's a straight-up combo of the two. My therapist really fucks with me about it. She says shit like: "Is it hard being one of the few black fag boys in a sea of white boys?" and "Is it hard being poor in such an affluent city?" and "Do you feel like these factors affect who you date/who will date you?" I always want to ignore questions about race and class because the true answers to these questions never seem to work in my favor, and also I feel like if I can just ignore it, it will (hopefully) all go away.

Those true answers are no less true than the answers I have come up with, those being: that I do *not* not fit in because I'm black; I do *not* not fit in because I'm poor; I don't fit in because I want to fucking kill and I want to find the boys that feel the same way I do; I know that they are out there.

I don't date anyone, and all the couples come in on Saturday night. I hate seeing couples because they make me feel lonely. I'm not discouraged overall, and I've fucked too many people's boyfriends to question my desirability, but my inner child won't let me not feel like something unfair and conspiracy-like is going on here. Maybe it's the way I dress. On my way to pick up a burger, I look in the full-length mirror on the way to the kitchen, and after dissing the clone boys I'm ready to admit some things about my fashion victimness. I dress like an asshole Berkeley student from some undecipherable decade midcentury. I hate nostalgia. I'm talking awkward glasses, anonymous black shoes, plain white tee, and fucking khakis. Like, who the fuck wears khakis? I basically dress like I did in grade school, and I'm now ready to forgive all the bullies for kicking my ass. I look like a dweeb. But if you dress like a nerd, people give you the once over and never really guess that you're falling apart on the inside. Or that you want to kill. Camouflage. Urban camouflage. The ultimate problem with dressing like a child from the sixties (and being black) is that you can say to yourself "I'm dressed classic American" or "I'm a modernist" or "I dress like the black dude in Weezer." The problem is that the rest of the world doesn't have that much art, and all those Eastern European/Australian/Midwestern/Clone Core tourist assholes who pollute the restaurant see is Urkel. Steven *fucking* Urkel. It always hurts. This bitch called me Urkel one night and I almost cried, but then I remembered that it was the future and I could certainly get away with slapping a white woman. I didn't though. Like, what if she slapped me back? What then? I had no time to entertain a standoff.

Fifteen assholes walk in the door and I have a panic attack. Ten more walk in behind them and, as is always the case in my life, I ignore my own emotional needs for a job well done. The rush leaves and then shit really hits the fan. Michael walks in with Johnny. Me and Johnny fucked a week ago and I even told him he didn't have to use a rubber so he would like me more. I felt bold enough to ask why he didn't call me and he said plain as uninked paper "Because his dick is bigger." I wanted to be mad but knew that you can't really argue with that reasoning. My mom had a saying for worrying about things you can't change: "Your arms are too short to box with God." Apparently, my dick was too.

Fuck this. I'm getting high. I bought some shitty coke from the cook, got off at 5:00 a.m., and went straight to the parking lot of the Travelodge in the Castro. But wait! This isn't shitty blow! This is good blow! Or speed? I've never felt like this. Sweating, short of breath, dick rock hard, and lonely. So fucking lonely. I meet this guy who looks like he's tried every drug ever offered to him. He takes me to a room in the Lodge that he's sharing with some other dude and that shit looks like a tornado had hit it. Nasty stuff everywhere, it looked like I could actually get bitten by a snake if I walked in. He says we don't have to stay and that he lives in the Fillmore. On the walk to his apartment I learn:

1. He's a drummer.
2. He's into jazz. *Really* into jazz.
3. He plays drums in a jazz band in Berkeley.

and

4. He likes to shoot up.

Before we walk into the apartment he casually says "I need to shoot up before we fuck." At first I pause out of modesty but then remembered that I can do whatever the fuck I feel like. It's too late to try to fuck someone else; this ship was sailing. He puts on a jazz record and dips his syringe into a cup of water and says "Don't drink out of this cup," and even with the very limited knowledge I have of his "lifestyle" I remember the thought bubble above my head reading *DUH BITCH*.

We started fucking and like the animal I am I got right the fuck *in there*. I was like "Yeah, take all that little dick ya fucking junkie. You ain't got no future and neither do I!" (giggling in my head like a little school girl the entire time) when all of a sudden he was like "My roommate lives down the hall. She's chubby. We can fuck her too." *Ewwwwwwww-www!!!!!!!! Did he really fucking just say that???* But then there's really no fuel left to be scandalized when your barebacking some junkie you just met. Fuck it. Charge it to the game. Or not. This dude was clearly an asshole. The sun had come up and he told me he liked the way I dressed and that we should be boyfriends. I took a mental survey of the scene around me. I was in the Fillmore with my junkie, jazz drummer boyfriend, fucking to jazz records dressed like an asshole Berkeley student from the fifties. Dude fuck that. That's some beatnik shit and *I hate* nostalgia. I ran out of the apartment completely naked.

EPILOGUE

Three days after Johnny told me he loved Michael more (because his dick was bigger) I began to get all affected. First I started binge eating, then I started cutting myself, then I took control. I did some yoga, rinsed out my ass, moisturized, put on a pair of black Calvin Klein mesh briefs, black Levi's skinny jeans, monochrome black Adidas, black gloves, black faux football face paint (like Left Eye from TLC — RIP) and a black skullcap. A gold chain and one diamond earring. I sprayed on some Calvin Klein OBSESSION. I either looked like a hip cat burglar or a member of the Black Bloc. It was time for justice. I got a black bag and put in a black rope with a grappling hook attached to the other end and a brick with a note attached. I snorted some X (left over from the night before) for a calming effect, and hopped on my bike en route to Johnny's apartment. I locked up my bike and shimmied up the side roof ladder to the top of the four-story apartment building, from there I took the grappling hook and rappelled down the side of the building till I was on the ground looking up at his second-story apartment window. (I could have just walked to the other side of the building from the sidewalk but I was addicted to the drama of the grappling hook.) I said a prayer to Ogun (the African god of war), and with solid aim and dexterity threw the brick through Johnny's window, laughing my ass off as I ran back to my bike. I imagined the look on Johnny's face when he took the note off the brick, revealing the message (written in

crayon) "JOHNNY WOULD YOU LOVE ME
IF MY DICK WERE BIGGER?"

(Two months later Johnny forgave me and
threw a brick through my window with a note
attached that said YES.)

WHY I AM A RESTAURANT WORKER

I really hate my therapist. Like, really. The subject of this session was supposed to be "Why I Am a Restaurant Worker" and why I can't find the inclination to switch to another line of work. But then, of course, the conversation degenerates into my absent father and how I was molested. Every session dissolves into my absent father and me being molested. So boring! (In the head of the therapist there was this invisible golden string that linked a profession where you're essentially performing to being an actual performer to this need for attention which goes back to my absent father and me being molested. ZZZZZZZZZZZZZZZZZZZ.) I can't believe I pay twenty-five dollars sliding scale just to be fucked with, but I do it cause none of my friends will listen to me bitch anymore so I have to pay someone. This is called "what the fuck?" I'd really only worked in restaurants, and ultimately knew it suited me best. I was a nervous soul. I never sat still much. I liked standing on my feet, being present and engaged with people (or charmingly aloof), and flirting with people for tips. Despite everything I knew about the world around me, I still had a genuine love for humankind (I wasn't sure how, I just felt lucky that I indeed did). I liked eye contact with strangers. I liked being a focal point. The times being what they were, everyone I knew was either a server, a bartender, bar back, hooker, porn star—sorry porn actor, or an office worker. I never really fucked with computers so I stayed in restaurant work 'cause that's where I started.

There was the barbecue and catfish restaurant many of my distant cousins worked at. Such and such barbecue that took its name from my hometown in Alabama. I could wear whatever I wanted there. The floor and kitchen were huge and a general sense of unruliness went. The restaurant was thirty years old and had two locations, one off the highway and one a mile and a half down (the original location). My family ate at the original every Sunday after church as a tradition. I worked at "the new one" as it was called. I was a busboy and prep. Every weekend I made upwards of eighty (fucking) gallons of sweet tea.

I leave reeking of buttermilk, onion powder, and cornmeal mix, or rather, hushpuppies—

what that combination is called when fried together. I get sexually harassed by this boy I went to kindergarten with before I switched schools; this big white mean redneck motherfucker. His nine-month-pregnant girlfriend worked in the kitchen with him, big-bellied, sliding on the greasy floor. I worry about her a lot. He's a dick. He calls me faggot a lot and always talks (specifically to me) about how big his dick is. This one time he gets me in the bathroom, turns out the lights, and grabs my dick. This other time while peeling onions in the kitchen, he slaps me in the nuts so hard I can't breathe and crouch down on the greasy, wet floor for a full minute. I was relieved when he left to join the army. (Though now, years later, I miss him every day.) It's in the same restaurant I meet Jamie. Jamie is this big ol' redneck girl. Six foot, 230, like big. Now as a teen, I am somewhat of a misfit, 265 pounds, five foot seven, nerd glasses, and this weird affected valley-girl accent from listening to too many Bikini Kill records. (I hold on to the accent cause it's a cool/useful way to disarm the redneck clientele.) Did I mention my child-bearing hips and girly ass? Not to toot my own horn, but I'm pretty fucking hot. Jamie loves me — especially my child-bearing hips and girly ass. Lesbians love that shit. Perverts. She can't keep her hands off of me. She always tells me how much she loves my child-bearing hips and girly ass and how hot I am. She tells me that I'm hot so much I actually start to believe it. It makes me slightly uncomfortable, but when you're young attention feels good and she's not some creepy dude. She says, "You know you're gay right?" And it makes everything okay. She talks a lot about getting fisted and I'm not really sure what she means. She checks out nearly everyone, and I remember wanting to be the type who could check out anybody. It seems romantic. She sneaks me into my first gay club at seventeen and that "do you think you're better off alone" song is playing. She drinks and fucks a lot. She's super Christian (somehow) and actually slaps me for saying goddamn this one time. We have so much in common. We're chubby, andro-ish, both abuse survivors, and both very, *very* stuck here. I often wonder what ever happened to her.

Every spring there are Civil War reenactments up the road near Tennessee. The participants eat at the restaurant afterwards as a tradition. I'm serving sweet tea to a room full of men dressed like Confederate soldiers and it hits me — *I have to get the fuck out of here*. I decide to move to Chattanooga. My last night of work, somehow (something that, years later, is still really unclear to me) a rumor gets spread through town and to my very Christian family that I'm joining a cult up by the Tennessee line near the mountains. My aunt comes one hour before my shift ends, and tells me I'm going to be institutionalized if I try to move away. One hour later thirteen members of my family show up with cameras and Bibles. I try to get into my friend's car and my family attacks me and my friends. I'm being pulled out of the car and my cousin is punching me in the neck. "Have you forgotten God? Have you forgotten how to pray?" she says as she's beating my ass. All the trashy waitresses are outside smoking and watching the whole thing. The cops show up and shit gets even more stupid. My mom relays her version of my life story to the cop, and the redneck asshole looks me up and down (in that "tsk tsk wayward son" kind of way) and says "Wish my son got to go to college for free" (I know what he secretly means by this, and it stands true to this day that I've never seen one red fucking cent from that United Negro College Fund). I know this peckerwood can fuck off, but I decide not to talk shit to the white man with the gun. Even in the face of all this trauma, I know this is all called "beside the point." I'm eighteen and allowed to go and my fearless punk friends, though beaten and harassed, are still waiting for me (even though the cops fucked with them), and this is why I still fuck with punks (in the good sense, not like the cops did) to this day. I remember thinking *Holy shit, I'm really out of here*. They deliver me to Chattanooga the next day and I immediately get a job at the Pickle Barrel—another fucking restaurant.

Today, my mom and family still laugh their asses off when someone asks "Whatever happened to your son who ran off with those white devil-worshippers?

MY GAY UNCLE

It was five minutes before 8:00 p.m.; I was almost done with my shift. Afterward I was to meet my uncle and his husband for dinner in the Western Addition. My uncle had worked in the same diner as me in the eighties. He had moved from Oakland when he was sixteen ("I was too girl for Oakland") and into an apartment at Eighteenth and Collingwood in the Castro. He said on a good Saturday night he could just wait on his second-story balcony until the bars let out and throw down his keys to cute passersby without saying a word. Sounded rad to me!

I felt weird. Two Sundays before I'd had dinner with him and his friends, my "other uncles" as he referred to them, and he specifically told me not to sleep with "Uncle Mike"—his best friend. I began to understand why. Uncle Mike waited until my real uncle was out of earshot, then began to tell me this other eighties (and current?) story of how he would put coke on the end of his dick (unbeknownst to the bottom) to numb the bottom so they could fuck longer. I kept it secret from my uncle that we had been fucking like crazy the past two weeks.

I got to dinner at my uncle's and that shit turned into a full-on character assault. My uncle asked me eight times during the course of dinner why I didn't have a boyfriend yet, and didn't I know that I wasn't getting any younger? I already had answers. Money. Time. My drinking problem. My fear of commitment. Also, I was already married—to my art. My gay uncle wasn't having it. Nine fuck buddies and not a single boyfriend tsk tsk. I tried to explain to him, this was sexual progress, this was revolution (this was all high risk). My gay uncle stated calmly: "You need to wash your pussy out and go find a man."

My mission was clear now:

1. Wash my pussy out.
2. Go find a man.

The last time I went on a date was 2006. This dude I was fucking invited me over to dinner with the other dude he was fucking and shit got blown to hell exponentially. The other kid had better musculature and liked to be called racial slurs when he was getting fucked. Like how the fuck was I supposed to compete with that? In an effort to outdo the other boy, I told my love interest he could fuck me in a Klansman outfit. We tried it for a couple of minutes, but my heart wasn't in it and love is not spelled with three K's; I learned the hard way. After that tawdry bullshit I decided to stop dating and just get fucked a lot. It was easier than trying.

"You should find a man like your Uncle _____" (his husband).

Tall, Polish. Dependable. Poland. Where the fuck is Poland?

I didn't have the heart to tell my uncle that I planned a future of gaining weight like my idol Aretha Franklin, owning twelve cats, and paying for sex with my disability checks. I'd be free to decide without some dude telling me what to do. Be it gym teacher, cop, or boyfriend, all authority figures bug the hell out of me. I wanted to be free of all the dumbness. FREE. DUMB. Freedom. "I give up on you," he says. His husband pats me on the shoulder, "You're at an impossible age to find a good husband. Just wait." He gets up to go sit at the opposite end of the dining room where there's a piano and plays (from memory no less) a forty-minute classical piece and actually cries in the middle of it, and maybe I do want to marry a man like my uncle. *Where the fuck is Poland?*

POSITIVE RESULTS

I was feeling rather AIDS-y. I had this recur-
ring nightmare where I'd go to the STD clinic,
say my name, and red lights would start flash-
ing and a siren would go off. I sat there with
my HIV counselor and told her my sexual history of the last year—and I swear to god she
did this—she got up, rolled her eyes (hard),
and said (valley girl accent) "Um, I think you
might be HIV positive." And she was right!
"How do you think this happened?" she asked.
I thought long and hard. It was probably one
of the couple hundred guys I let nail me without a rubber, but I didn't say that because even
though I didn't really know this bitch, I still,
for some reason, didn't want her to think I
sleep around. "I caught it from a toilet seat."

She didn't laugh. I sensed she was a dyke
and there is no way you're ever going to convince a lesbian that semen is cool. Unless she's
trying to get pregnant, that is. Nuh-uh, for-

get it! I did the same thing I always did when cornered, I lied through my fucking teeth. "I caught it from my monogamous boyfriend who was cheating on me (sniff, sniff)." Now she was ready to treat me like a human being. "Oh honey! Here's some tissue! The world is so unfair! That monster!" I kinda hate this bitch, and how come there's no sympathy for sluts? Like none? What if I had told the truth? "Oh, I just wanted to be liked." She would have certainly labeled me a menace to society. "Here's some condoms and lube," she said. I took the lube. I was rather traumatized by the news. I mean, I didn't wanna cry or throw things. To be honest, I mostly just wanted some orange juice. I wasn't going to cry, but I was definitely gonna do some Oxycodone. I called my cousin back home in tears, "Roscoe, I have HIV (sniff, sniff)," to which he responded, "Oh, like Magic Johnson? Fuck it nigga! Just eat some vegetables!" I had to slow down his words in my head, "Fuck it nigga, just eat some vegetables." Sound advice! But I never eat vegetables or drink water. I eat coffee. I'm definitely going to die. Or something. I remember sitting in the STD clinic and looking at a model of HIV. Ugly thing. It looked like something off of *Star Trek*. A glob-shaped thing with red dots all over it. Plugs itself into one of your cells and makes hella copies of itself. Despite my number of partners, I had a good idea of who did this to me. I didn't let a lot of guys cum in me. (Just ones I thought were hot.)

He lived up the street. When I biked up to meet him and told him, he said "Well, this is going to be hard now that I'm seeing someone I actually care about . . ." And what was I, chopped liver? But wait, I *was* chopped liver. We met online and his pic was of him naked with his bare ass up in the air; and I'm certain that if there really is a hell, all us gay boys are going for how carelessly we treat each other. Perhaps. After I tell him, we sit on his bed crying and holding each other for forty minutes, and it strikes me that even though we've been fucking for months this here is the most intimate thing we've ever done with one another. I take a long look at him. Big ol' white boy, Scandinavian descent (I could never quite pronounce his last name right). Six foot four, 220 pounds (all muscle), blond hair, blue eyes. Looked like he had sailed over from Scandinavia that day on a Viking boat with twenty of his horny cousins. I get a hard on and ask if he wants to fuck one last time. I had already exhausted my risk, like, why the fuck not? He laughs and kicks me out and calls his new boyfriend to inform him that he might have quite possibly ruined his life. I biked away knowing I would never see him again, and despite

25

everything, I know this is not some great trag-edy. ("I don't believe that!" says a boy in writ-ing class. "I don't believe it when you say it was no great tragedy!" I assure him that that particular day, it indeed wasn't.)

I snort some Oxycodone and then take a shit. There's something totally shamanistic about taking a shit on drugs. I sat on the toi-let all itchy and sweaty, and my mind went to dark places. I caught visions of my last two t-cells sitting on a couch in my bloodstream smoking crack, when all of a sudden one of them looks at the other and is like "Dude, fuck this place," and they both shoot themselves in the head! The rope attaching me to Earth is cut, and I go flying UP UP UP above the world. I high-five my dead great-grandmother ("Wel-come," she says lovingly). I'm really high. I willfully switch the vision. I know I want to be an old man. I picture myself on the seven acres of land my father leaves for me in Alabama. I'm sitting on my big plantation-house porch in a rocking chair, long white/gray hair, smok-ing weed, house full of hot young boys—and old ones too—growing organic watermelons and shit. Yes. I get up to wipe, and I'm so high I stare at my shit on the toilet paper for like, two hours. When that wears off, I go and cook myself some vegetables.

SHIT, POOP DICK, VOMIT, AND OTHER UNFORTUNATE CIRCUMSTANCES

There was shit everywhere in the city. "I don't mind it if it's on my dick!" as the saying goes, but it was *everywhere*. This junkie took a shit by my doorstep, not in polite little logs, but in one huge ominous bulb that rounded at the top and sides like a three-pound mushroom. To add insult to injury, the culprit took a toy candy dispenser (called "The Sweet Machine") and (strategically?) stuck it down in the center of the shit. I cleaned it on my way to work and all day I could fell the heavy shit stank fume in my lungs. I put the shit-covered Sweet Machine in a bag by the garbage cans on the street. It disappeared for two hours and then someone brought it right back. What horrible thing had I done to deserve this? I got to the restaurant late. Again. The only customer was a junkie too. I didn't know this until he passed out at the table for thirty minutes. I walked by and caught a whiff of him and he had totally shit himself. I moved to a safer place in the restaurant, and from afar saw him wake up, knock over his water, reach his finger in the back of his pants, SMELL IT, freak out, and run to the restroom. He stayed in the restroom for thirty more minutes, and when he came out (doing that whole "I'm on heroin" nod off thing) the toilet and sink were completely covered in feces. (He hands me ten dollars for his milkshake — which I immediately soak in alcohol.) Later that day in writing class the teacher asks us to write about unpleasant things and I title mine "Shit, Poop Dick, Vomit, and Other Unfortunate Circumstances."

1. I brought this one asshole home from the bar and we fucked like drunk people. Then, of course, I had to pay the toll. I pulled out of him, dick dirty, and the room filled with the smell of curried vegetables. He almost threw up and I tried to say soothing and attentive top things like "Don't worry baby, it's human — it's natural" (even though I wanted to fucking *die*). I wiped my dick on a dirty sock and threw it under my bed. The weird part: three months later, when I cleaned my room, I couldn't find the poop sock anywhere. What happened?

2. What is extraordinary is that I had known this boy a full eight years before we boned. A

precedent of sorts but then it still all turned to hell. He wanted to fuck in the morning. I hate morning sex. The morning is not a sexy time. It's all about the beer shit, bad breath, that bloated gassy feeling, hunger pangs—couldn't you just make love to my mind? "No way," he says. I'd rather hate myself than fuck in the morning, but to make *him* happy I give in and bend over. Normally I just shut up and internalize my bottom role, but I couldn't move past the rather pessimistic thought/fact that getting fucked in the ass when you're not feeling it is so demeaning. Whatever. That's when my lover (that big dick mule) pulled out and *ow!* It felt like he yanked out a kidney! I looked to see if I had left any guts on his dick and I had! This brownish-red crown "crowned" the head of his dick. It was like murder! Then he just sat there *smiling* no less! He carelessly plopped down on the bed and smeared the remnants of my lower intestines on the sheet, didn't say a word and even checked his email with my shit still on his dick. I judged him, showered, and left. I mean, I guess it's a bit hypocritical to be fecalphobic if you're going to fuck people in the ass, but why did it all just seem so wrong to me? I knew we could never be together because he was too comfortable with my shit.

3. At the end of the day I have to say my most impressive sex partners have always been druggy, straight punk boys 'cause they don't give a fuck. I don't want shaved butthole gay dude sex because I'm an (unapologetic) self-loathing gay. Just saying. Anywho, we smoked (yes smoked) half an eighth of shrooms, ate the other half, and he started fucking my face. Oops! Too much air! I threw up on the side of the bed and floor. He gently caressed my face and said "Awww, baby!" threw a towel over the vomit, and we started fucking again. Ew.

4. I was fully engaged in sexual intercourse with a silver fox flight attendant thirty years my senior. Very suddenly my dick popped out of him, slapped against my stomach, and I could see (in the moonlight-drenched room) this huge angry shit-ball roll, sticky slow, down my stomach and onto the floor. When we turned the lights on I couldn't see the shit-ball anywhere! I think the dog ate it.

EXPERIMENTAL (PORNO),
TRASH, AND NO STAR

1. My first boyfriend in San Francisco was a total motherfucker. There I was in some random backyard, freezing, in a shit-ton of makeup, about to do my first unicorn porn. The question was not *Why am I doing this?* but rather *Why am I doing this for free?!* But wait. I know why. In my twenty-two-year-old reasoning, I was doing this because I wanted him to love me back. Buh-buh-buh-bullshit. Some people say love doesn't cost a thing, but I equate love to a credit card or a loan from the mafia, i.e., you'll always pay much more later. Getting fucked by a unicorn wasn't so much morally taxing as physically taxing. The horn was pointy as fuck and it made me bleed. Years later, coked out in a bathroom stall, me and my director boyfriend argued over the physical logistics of getting fucked in the ass. "There should be that point where you don't feel anything," he said. The problem was that

I felt everything, and that was the core of our disagreement. He was a power bottom; I was a power(less) bottom. We mutually didn't get it. The day I left the set I called my mother and asked "Oh Mama! Was I exploited?" "Probably," she said. "But think about it like this baby. There are some sick fucks in the world. Some people fuck animals. Some people fuck children. But fucking a unicorn . . . that's art." And with that well-placed advice I decided to chill the fuck out on it. I am still charmed and even bewitched when I see my old boyfriend, though we don't spend much time talking about our old "art film."

2. I got picked to be in an indie-rock-boy skin flick. The plot concerned various boys in SF looking for love and there would be cum shots and boners—very avant-garde. I played a retail employee and a top (two things I despise more than anything, but I wanted a role that challenged me). The cast got together and had a meeting. We saw this movie as a political strategy. We wanted to challenge gay male body image bullshit, and all decided to grow our hair and gain thirty pounds each. Since we all had no body hair to speak of we defined ourselves as "cherubs" (i.e., chubby yet hairless or chubby wubby wasn't fuzzy, was he?). Only time would tell if the bear community

would accept us as their hairless cousins or if they were gonna be total stuck-up bitches about it (as bears usually are. Let's face it).

I showed up to the first day of shooting plump as fuck, looking like an indie-rock version of Rerun from *What's Happening!!*, and the rest of those sluts were still skinny! Turns out they thought I was just joking. I could have killed those cunts, but their skinny bodies would just taste like macrobiotic food. Fuck that. I had no choice but to go on. At the movie premiere I was shocked to find out how fucking good I look on camera with thirty extra pounds. The extra weight filled in all my drug wrinkles! Not to mention the "weight" it added to my sex scenes. I sucked dick and ate ass like a hungry person and the audience applauded. After leaving the movie premiere I ate a whole bucket of fried chicken and high-fived *myself*, thanking the Goddess that the world around me was perhaps ready for this jelly.

3. Nudity. I got asked to be naked on the cover of one of the free weekly papers, and I said yes 'cause I'm that type of ride-or-die bitch. I also felt like someone had to represent for the uncircumcised community, plus no matter how much I try to be hard, I am in fact a total fucking hippie. Like in my head's happy place

I'm running around naked in a big-ass sunny field, with a sunflower in my ass, totally *feeling it*. It went to newsstands and it made this one sister I know react: "Why was the white dude's dick bigger? Do you think it was a racial conspiracy?" (She was going hard with this.) And I was like "Naw dude. Genetics?" We dropped it and got high and went to Whole Foods.

AN INTERVENTION

I had moved from the graveyard to the morning shift. Seven a.m. I had to leave Oakland
by 6:00 a.m. five days a week. I begin to notice
this was equally as taxing as the graveyard in
that damned if you do, damned if you don't
kinda way. This crazy old lady came in, hip as
fuck, with a manicured 'do—how did a homeless woman have such fabulous hair? Is that
classist to ask? Either way, she kept dumping
quarters and breaking up cigarettes in her coffee and pouring it all over the table. Twenty
minutes after kicking her out, I regretted it
'cause it left me alone in the restaurant with
my acute depression, which had been going
on for two and a half years.

This depression had begun after I left the
diner to go to Europe and came back to find
that they had given my job away. I went to
work at this pizzeria in Berkeley. Kinda sucked.
I got hit on by weirdo, bisexual Berkeley soc-

cer dads, and I hated being a dishwasher. The job was dangerous for a couple of reasons: it was close to a bar that gave discounted drinks to the employees of the pizza place and it was four blocks away from the bathhouse. I sometimes came to from blackouts walking around in there. One night I was so bored I snuck a fifth of Jack into work, got blackout drunk, got into an argument with the closing manager, and got fired. It was the third job I had lost to drinking—so I was used to it! Whatever. And whoever gave a fuck about washing dishes anyway? Losing the job didn't break my heart—coming to at the bathhouse did though. I got to a point where even when not blackout (just slightly buzzed) I'd still let basically anyone fuck me, like that eighty-year-old who always wore the aviator goggles, Raphael the blind poet, and any number of bathhouse employees. It was before I was positive, and I felt like I was going to have to fight like hell to maintain my negative status 'cause either I liked fun too much or had a death wish (it was hard to discern). My therapist at the time told me to write a story about everything that happened to me while working at the pizzeria. "Pay close attention to the actions of the boy in that story," she said. "Can you live with the boy in that story?"

I couldn't live with the boy in that story. I felt

like I had failed myself. I countered by attending Barebackers Anonymous meetings. The meetings were usually full. We were all substance addicts of some sort. Junkies, drunks, tweekers, you name it. I regret to admit that, in the beginning, I had a slight prejudice against the tweekers. As the saying goes, a junkie will steal your shit. Period. A drunk will steal your shit and forget about it. But a tweeker will steal your shit and then help you look for it. I couldn't always discern which was worst, but I let my guard down and learned to love my tweeker brothers. As we revealed our lives in stories, it turned out I had done *waaaaay* sketchier shit blackout drunk than most of them pulled being up for six days. Judge not, I learned. I also learned other useful things in Barebackers Anonymous, like how pulling out is, in fact, not a form of disease prevention, and how to turn down a piece of ass every once in a while. This drastic-ass old stunt queen had this awesome story about how in the midnineties in a sex club in Amsterdam, she stayed up on tweak and took 112 anonymous loads of cum up her butt in one four-hour "sitting" (she had been up for two weeks), and how, besides the speed part, she regretted *nothing*. 112 loads. Shit fuck Jesus Mary. Who was keeping count?! This story became no less compelling when she told it . . . *every meeting*. I remember thinking it wasn't hot in a porny way, more like an Animal Channel kind of way. I remember this one time she told that story and it made me throw up my tuna fish sandwich. The only time I called bullshit was when this Financial District asshole talked for forty-five minutes straight (leaving five minutes in the session for the rest of the group) about his raging speed addiction and had the nerve to say "I'm too rich not to be happy . . ." (I almost barfed.) I too, being rich (if only in spirit), showed up stoned, crashed somewhere in the middle of this dude's buh-buh-buh-bullshit soliloquy, and in the post-stoned sober haze realized "Wait a minute, that bitch is still tweaking!" The piece of shit psychology major intern that was facilitating hadn't even caught that shit, and I was feeling judgmental (I had certainly been pushed), and wrote in the suggestion box to him at the end of group "You're an asshole and you should kill yourself." Then, just to be a total bitch, asked that selfsame asshole in the lobby outside group if I could borrow twenty dollars.

THE ASSIGNMENT
OR
JOHNNY WOULD YOU LOVE ME IF
MY DICK WERE BIGGER: PART 2

As part of our treatment process in Bareback-ers Anonymous we had to complete weekly assignments. Assignment #1: Go buy some condoms you dirty whore. I went to the drug store and stared at the box of condoms that were my size (i.e., snugger fit). It dawns on me that I didn't catch HIV because I was whoreishly promiscuous (per se), I caught HIV because I was too embarrassed to buy size snugger-fit condoms. Bummer. To add insult to injury Michael was in there buying condoms too! He was walking around with a box of XL-size Magnums! Smiling no less! On my way to the bathroom to kill myself, I saw a pack of mango chili peppers. It brought on memories that got me thinking about the com-plexities of the question of dick size.

1. I was hanging out with Texas. Texas is a big ol' white boy from Brooklyn. He's hung like a

(well-hung) Puerto Rican. After a recent trip to Thailand, he reported that the native boys throw themselves at white tourists under the assumption that they: a. have bigger wieners and b. more money (though personally I feel like when it comes to faggot shit fuckery, money is always a bigger motivation—maybe I'm just a greedy bitch—anywho). Texas also reported that the native tops, acclimating to this fucked-up cultural annoyance, developed a saying: "Why have big banana when you could have hot chili pepper?" Hot. Chili. Pepper. 'Cause that's what a little one feels like! How sensory! I knew I was mentally ill because this story made me feel better.

2. I worked at a strip joint for a bit as a jizz-mopper. I also walked the girls back and forth to the booth to make sure they didn't get harassed. Me and this Russian stripper-girl used to talk it up all the time especially about dicks. One time she said (spy accent), "I think all guys should have their dick size tattooed on their foreheads." At first the raging bottom in me was like "Fuck yeah . . ." but the humanitarian in me kicked in "Wait a minute, that's some Nazi Germany shit!" All I could imagine was that one guy walking around with a negative two on his forehead talking about "At least I'm pretty." Bummer.

3. I was staying with a friend in New York and she asked me to pick her up some tampons and Magnum condoms for her boyfriend. I wanted to explore what it was like, so I walked around CVS for twenty minutes holding them so people would notice. No one gave a shit, especially the lady who rang me up who looked like she hadn't had sex since the Civil War. She eyeballed me in this certain kind of way and then announced over the loudspeaker that she needed a price check on the enemas I was buying, put it all in the bag, and said "Have a good day, sir." I took all these mental notes, walked right up to Michael, and asked him on a date. We went to see his friend's band play and fucked at his house (with condoms!). I also learned that despite having, like, five pounds of dick he's a raging bottom. I fucked him. We get pizza after, and I save the chili pepper packets, and just to be *really* obtuse mail them to him the next day. I report to my Barebackers Anonymous group that I had used a condom (everyone applauded) and that I felt like I was well on the road to recovery. But that's about the time That Asshole joined the group and everything fell to hell . . .

HOW TO SURVIVE SHITTY MEN AND HOW TO SURVIVE BEING A SHITTY MAN*

(*There was a nonfiction writing contest for an up-and-coming gay youth magazine for male-identified youth, i.e., little faggots [fagettes?], age fourteen to twenty-four. The contest called for a sort of "how-to" guide for entering/surviving adult gay life. I saw that shit, giggled a little, and submitted "How to Survive Shitty Men/ How to Survive Being a Shitty Man" and was promptly rejected . . .)

1. That Asshole. I'll start by saying that the end of my friendship with That Asshole marked the official start of my two-and-a-half year depression. To this day, I have no clue why he had even showed up to Barebackers Anonymous since he wasn't trying to change. Pretty soon I was skipping meetings to fuck around with him. I was struck. He wasn't a big guy. Super fair. Big blue eyes. Intense, but delicate despite himself. He had an acid tongue

to match. That little bitch had smelly breath not from the cottonmouth from all the weed he smoked, but simply because of all the shit he talked. He was pretty to look at, and the icing on the cake was that he actually lisped. Like, not ironic, not affected, but a surefire 100 percent big ol' "I'm a queer — bash me" lisp. I thought it was one of the sexiest things about him. Though I was in my early twenties, I had some hardline politics about who I was attracted to. I didn't give a flying fuck about "masculine" men. I wanted a faggot. Like a total fucking flamer with a tank full of sugar. Someone who understood fully what the fuck I had to go through in the world. Midfriendship he got married to a wonderful man who dressed really butch. He started to dress really butch. By this time, I saw him as a big brother who I looked up to. We started fucking more when I started dressing more butch. I was still too young when he said he wanted to fuck me but didn't want to use condoms, ever. I was taken aback. Sometimes I would get blackout and tell the wrong people about it. Now, he was pretty buck. Went to anonymous hotel sex parties, did bareback porn — like he was really going for it. I, at the time, was still hanging out in the shallow end of the pool, and when he said he wanted to fuck me raw it sounded like a challenge. Looking back, I felt like what we had going was tantamount to a suicide pact. I learned later (as we too often do) that fucking all the time isn't always based in "celebrating life." It can sometimes be depression, sometimes mania, whichever. I would one day look back to see what basically was going on was two boys, misfits of sorts, accessing masculinity through sex because raw sex was "how men do it," alongside the fact that it felt good. I gave in to his demand 'cause the thought of him not loving me or not wanting to have sex with me was scarier than any disease. It was just that pathetic, that simple, and that stupid. It started rather innocently at first. In the years that followed, he moved away for a bit, and I started getting fucked at the bathhouse without condoms too often. Started feeling new things. Like the feeling of fucking some guy who already had some other guy (or several guys) cum in them. All of the fluids mixing—it turned me on something terrible, but I never talked or wrote about it 'cause that type of thing would get you labeled a hoodlum. I went sober for a couple of years and could no longer blame my favorite pastime on alcohol or anyone but myself anymore. I look back and reason that I was trying to get back that first feeling or experience, as most addicts do. I looked for That Asshole in pieces of strangers, be it the weight of them on top of me or the intensity of eye contact while they were fucking me. It was always different because they weren't my best friend.

He moved back and said we could be together, like boyfriends. He lied. I remember all hell breaking loose the night he asked me to sleep on the couch — it was clear he'd changed his mind. I don't really blame him. He hated my drinking and made me promise I would quit. I lied. Me and him were both in the habit of making promises we couldn't possibly keep. In the time he was away, I did the whole bar thing and got rejected by quite a few guys. Keep in mind, these were guys he would fuck sometimes, but I was sworn to the secret code of best-buddyhood and could never let the cat out of the bag that we fucked sometimes. It made me hateful and jealous. In our youth, we believed we could be fairy free — be best friends and fuck — but we learned that few men you were trying to date would ever accept that arrangement. My ego couldn't take it. Dealing with him made me learn what an evil cunt I could be. The night he made me sleep on the couch, I left, came back, and circled his car for an hour trying to resist the urge to bust out all his car windows. I started leaving abusive blackout messages on his answering machine. I was never too repentant about the messages though, I mean, at least it took me nine drinks to be a dick. He could do it stone-cold sober. Eventually I saw it for what it was: two young men that loved each other, but would always be too crazy to take care of each other the way we needed to. It seems I waited for years to hear him say "I'm your boyfriend." It certainly didn't have to be traditional; I just wanted to hear him say it. He never did and sometimes I still sit up too late at night inking up pages wondering if I miss him or not. This is what broke my heart . . .

2. I went to dinner with my boyfriend at the time and that shit turned into a full-on class war. He paid for everything, yet again. But oh no, this time he was juuuuust wasted enough to be a bitch about it. "Where is your money?! You never have any money!!!" There was this irritation in his tone and I knew he meant business. It was hard for me to give a fuck, why didn't he just date a lawyer? Or drug dealer? Or something . . . Saying "My artist boyfriend is always broke" is like saying "The sky is blue" or "The ocean is full of fish." Clearly tattooed on the forehead of such statements is "DUH BITCH." It wasn't the first time he'd emasculated me in public. Truthfully, he had to have been one of the most castrating men I had ever loved. I was used to turning diplomat: "Let's go home, baby." I stayed at his

house often to avoid my punk warehouse and ten roommates back in Oakland. "Home?!" he said queerly. "No. I have a home, you go back to your *homeless shelter* . . ." I smacked my fist against a newspaper stand, and when that didn't satisfy, drew my hand back and punched him in the face. He fell down, nose bleeding. I know I will regret it forever, but cannot deny the three immediate seconds of silence after: how peaceful they were and how good it felt to finally shut that nagging bitch the fuck up.

3. Pillow Talk and War Stories: It was always the boys that liked to lie in bed. I remember sitting up late at night trying to exorcise ghosts of dudes from the past. All men leave you with something different. Charles was buck. I liked Charles. Big ol' white boy from down South ("Rammerjammeryellowhammer, Give 'em hell Alabama!" as he'd say). In bed, he'd tell me stories about his trashy (and awesome) mom. As the story goes, his stepdad would go away on business trips and his mother would have sex with her boyfriend in his car at the end of their street. Whenever Charles's stepfather would call from the Midwest or up North or wherever he was, Charles's job was to flick the porch light on and off all flashy like, signaling his mother to come and take the call. Charles

explained that as he got older he began to "suffer" from the same "fever" as his mother.

There was Mickey. He also liked to lie in bed. His stories were grim; his dad had molested him. I remembered never feeling like I could protect him. He eventually went crazy on drugs and his mom came to get him and said she had no idea why he was so disturbed. I confronted her about the abuse.

I remember lying in the bed most with Jesse. He was the one I stayed in bed the longest with. I still remember the night where he, yet again, explained why I sucked at giving massages and why we shouldn't be friends that fuck around. Ever. No, like ever. Alongside telling me that I gave the best head ever. Like, ever. Whatever. Pillow Talk. War Stories. The men I've shared mental space with still keep me up at night. Most people count sheep to fall asleep. I just counted all my men.

4. The Disappearing Man: He woke up feeling invisible again. There was no excuse for him except he was over it and born over it. The days following the breakup were hard, and this particular day everything was bugging the fuck out of him. He woke up to rain and he was instantly over it. Plip. Plop. Plip. Plop. Plip . . . It was the squishy sound of soggy black sensible canvas shoes in the rain. This was the

beat that propelled him down the street to the bus, to the train, though he'd rather be home sleeping. When he left the house and went down the street, no one cheered, there was no celebration of roses. Just the morning call from his mother to remind him that Jesus loved him and that he was beautiful. *Well at least some-one loves me*, he thought. There were so many mistakes to think about on the train. Liquor bottles were piling up in his room and each seemed to have some sort of separate spiritual baggage attached. The night he had ruined his life this way, and how another night he ruined his life this other way. All the bottles denoted these failures, and keeping the bottles was evil magic that he did not fear. He was either bored or numb. He pontificated on the night everything had gone wrong. He'd had too many pills, trying to get through a party where the ex would be. Blackout. He heard the next morning that he was in the middle of the floor of the party crying and saying, "I gave _____ AIDS!"

He hadn't really given the boy AIDS, and he knew that. Was it the guilt of having sex with him in the first place (considering their serodis-cordant relationship) that caused a freak out, or the evil-bitch side that just wanted to fuck with an ex more? (The two men had hurt each other very often, with a fucked ease as if they were playing a game of tag.) It was yet another relationship lying on the floor busted to all hell in a million fucking pieces. It was everybody's fault. It started raining harder, and the moisturizer he used in the winter slipped off his skin and onto the pavement, mixing in the gutter with the incandescent pools of escaped motor oil, all sweeping down in the drain that goes to the bay, which goes to the ocean . . . At least he was clean. He moved defiantly forward. He didn't fear the rain. He knew it was only water. This is how he pleasantly (yet not so pleasantly) became translucent in the rainy and gray mornings that would come in his life at times. If you stood still behind him while he was walking down the street, you would notice that as he walked away, he seemed to disappear.

5. Me vs. the Writer: It was, of course, a mistake to date another writer. We differed and disagreed stylistically, and very, very often. He felt like I was too often sincere and forthcoming in my writing, and I thought he was too often full of shit. I took writing night classes, and he went to proper school for it so I tended to take his criticism to heart. He was often published in that *New Best Gay Erotic Fiction* volume what-the-fuck-ever, those books I tended to avoid. All of his stories were about

the "Incredible Adventures of Two Boring-Ass White Dudes in Love," and people actually *bought* that shit with money and belief. Hook. Line. Sinker. Not surprising really, most people eat at McDonald's. I just hated the plucky, wide-eyedness of it all. Like, why couldn't one of the precious boys be a murderer and a junkie or have an eating disorder? Anything to sex up and jazz up those boring-ass stories. I patted myself on the back for writing about real shit, like gun violence and semen addiction. Shit hit the fan the day I broke into his computer and was reading his journal, emails, and first drafts. Right there, in the middle of the screen, plain as a ten-inch boner, was something too familiar to me. He had stolen one of my ideas and put it in his own story. I knew he'd get paid for this story. The emasculation of it ripped right through me. War. War. War. Now, looking back, I think we were jealous of each other. I remember sometimes (sorta) envying his success or rather, wishing I was him; maybe my idea popping up in his story was him wishing he was me.

I was enraged. I took his laptop to the garden out back and poured lighter fluid (holy water) on it and set that silver bullshit on fire. He never talked to me ever again and he could never really return the favor — my stories were already on fire.

THE POLITICS OF BUG CHASING

I joined the online barebacking site 'cause I was out of ideas. The guy came over; he was on a five-day speed binge. He looked me in the eyes and told me he was worried about me. "Were you a bug chaser too?" he asks. I pause 'cause it's so rare I feel scandalized by something—I like the feeling. "Like, did I try to catch HIV on purpose?" *Hmmmmmmm*. I always have a hard time with that particular question. We fags are funny. We sit in church, point fingers, call ourselves stupid and cry ourselves to sleep at night over the subject of sex. Stupid is as stupid does (of course), and if you do it more than three times it's not a mistake anymore. The bug chaser says, "I'd rather have it so I can stop worrying about it." This is called "extreme." Looking back (with glasses) at certain jacked decisions in the past, I think it's also extreme to say, "I wanna do hella sketchy shit and don't want anything bad to happen." Passive acceptance is a motherfucker and maybe there isn't as much space between me and this guy as I thought. It took me three hours to kick him out because I couldn't stop fucking him. Now I know it's not a question of "Who's right, me or him?" We are both, of course, dead wrong. But the ultimate question is, who's more wrong?

TOUR DIARIES: TEXAS

1. Solange: It was the best of states. It was the worst of states. It was the best state of mind. It was the worst state of mind. It was South by Southwest and I couldn't (Kim) deal with it. It was a club situation. Me and this sister with an Afro did shrooms and went to the dying New York party that was doing a one-off nightclub in Austin that night. Ill Shapes or Cross Shapes or whatever with shapes (the name eludes me). We figured we better not cause too much trouble in the land of scary-ass white people, or Middle America as they call it, but we did, of course, and we paid the bullshit toll. I was with my bandmates and crew. We all look so good people wanna fuck with us and beat our asses. This Barbie pulled off my bandmate's hat so I, knee-jerk reaction style, ripped her (tacky) white patent leather clutch purse from under her arm and threw it across the room. In doing so, her phone must have fallen out. She

went to security and was like "that shirtless, high *black guy* stole my phone!" Oh shit! Right about that same time I looked over and see this cuuuute little high-yellow black girl dancing kinda close. She wants a faux vogue battle. She bewitches me. *Who is this cute little black girl?! Why is she dressed like Adam Ant?* (Complete with eight kinds of Burberry and a neon turquoise painted raccoon strip across her eyes — keep in mind neon turquoise as opposed to Adam's white one . . .) Wait a minute! THAT'S SOLANGE!!!!! Beyoncé's younger sister and black America's new neo-soul, crossover indie mistress. Yaaaaaas! I saw her a couple of months ago in SF with Estelle; she covered "Lovefool" by the Cardigans and I decided I would gladly follow her to hell — if need be. "HEY GIRL!" (I exclaim, as if I knew her). She came up dancing and we cut a mini rug. She asked how it was going and unfortunately the shrooms were acting as truth serum, "I'm getting kicked out of the club 'cause I threw some white girl's purse across the room." She looked at me as if I were a shirtless, high black guy who just said "I'm getting kicked out of the club 'cause I threw some white girl's purse across the room." One of her friends came to rescue her right as the big white police guy and black bouncer came to take me and my crew out. Shit show. Barbie starts yelling bullshit, the sister with an Afro spits in Barbie's face (I loved her for that) and I didn't get in too much trouble 'cause I remember the police treating me as if I was too gay to fuck with. ("That's right officer. I'm not gay. I'm just really, really HIGH.") Besides meeting Solange, that was some kind of bullshit. But that too would be ripped away. I was relating this story to T'Kwa (this angry ass African girl) and she was like "Beyuuuunnncé? Solaaaaaaaage? You hear that *French bullshit* in their names? Faggot, them is light-skinned creole girls from Texas, they don't represent us; hell yeah she looked at you crazy in the club, hell, she probably sided with that blond bitch! Look at how Kelly has to live!" I noticed me and T'Kwa, both broke as fuck, eating cereal, purple-tinted skin in colorful asymmetrical clothes. We looked like Nigerian new-wavers. I decided not to tell T'Kwa that whenever I looked in the mirror all I saw was a beautiful, skinny, high-yellow girl. I decided it was better to not be so forthcoming for once. I didn't want to get my ass beat by a politically convicted black girl. They are generally not kidding, and I decided to go ahead and take it up the ass. (Ass always.) "Sure," I said to T'Kwa. "Sure." (I saw Solange at SF Pride two years later and gave two snaps to the Goddess when I heard her say: "I gave up my spot at the BET Awards today to be with my people today." I recommitted my plan to follow her straight to hell, if need be.)

2. Long story short, we were diving around Texas in what we called "The Fag Clown Car." Two bands. One an all-fag rap group. My band was more new wave. We stopped at a Dairy Queen in Texas. The three girls in the van get out. No problem. The four other tattooed white fags get out. Hmmmm, a little challenging but par for the course. Then I get out. In all my Wesley Snipes–ean glory, wearing a peppermint-print tank top and jogging shorts that fall just below my nuts. Oh shit. Definitely can't ignore that. Those rednecks in the parking lot got predictably pissed. They may or may not have had guns (the story changes depending on who is telling it). We hightail it out of there and at the truck station at the very next stop, a horny trucker who seemed to love the way I dressed got me into a stall and came in my mouth when I asked him not to. Fuck Texas. Long live Texas.

SCIENCE FICTION/
COMPETITION FICTION

It was a Tuesday night and it was raining again. I was stuck at the diner. I had to miss writing class because I got called in to work. I was rather pissy about it and, to make myself feel better, ignored these two old broads who had shuffled in and been rude to me. They had been waiting twenty minutes and would continue to wait because I was over them. I had suspected for some time that my boss was a coke head . . . or something. He came in fake-tanned and wearing only tropical colors carrying a big-ass box that read "Popular Science Magazine"; the other side read "August '89– Sept '93." "Here," he said, "I found these in my garage and thought you might like them," and then leaves in a hurry. Naturally, I'm like *What the fuck?* A roach climbed out of the box and I was certain this box should have never been in a restaurant. Health code much? So little made sense in this place that I felt, for consistency's sake, I'd better not question anything. The icing on the cake was this would be an excellent way to ignore those rude old bitches more. I flip through the back ads of the December '91 issue and find a science fiction writing contest. This of course seemed like a dare, and I put pen to dinner napkin ('cause I didn't have notebook paper) with incredible results . . .

1. Womanhood: I met Armani on the last train car. Archetypal big, black, Mandingo-looking motherfucker. These genes had skipped me. He had what later measured out to be (I know this because he actually measured it in front of me, for *some* reason) nine inches of dick. Ow! My insides! "Do you want me to take these nine inches of dick and turn you into a woman?" he said. I mean I hadn't planned on it, but since I was already here, well, why the fuck not? I followed him to his government-subsidized apartment and let him fuck me spread-eagle on his kitchen cutting board. He was hitting it from the back when all of a sudden I spontaneously grew a ponytail, titties, and nine-inch acrylic nails. *Holy shit!* Armani came and was like, "Do not use this new gift for evil," and then his cryptic ass disappeared in a cloud of smoke. When he told me he was going to take his nine inches of dick and turn me into

a woman he, like, meant it. Being a woman ruled. In my everyday fag life I had dressed like a really dapper lesbian, but now that I was a woman I really turned it out and dressed like a drag queen. I'm talking weave down to my ass, ass and lashes for days, and pussy pinker than a honky. Can we talk about my pussy? Defiantly unshaven, it twinkled every time I spread my legs. But of course, the stress of the Modern Woman had not changed since the beginning of time. Like, what if I got pregnant? And worse still, what if I get pregnant by a poor person? Ew! Just like my mom! Whatever. I dodged the pregnancy bullet by only doing anal. That was, until I realized that vaginal sex was a fucking goldmine. My crowning achievement as a woman was mastering the abortion scam (that's where I pretended to get pregnant, demanded money for an abortion, and then blew it all on shoes). This one snarky fucker demanded a blow job after I picked up my fake abortion money. I laughed in his face. Stupid motherfucker. Didn't he know that I didn't have to suck dick, 'cause I have a pussy?

2. Jordy and the Scientologists: Jordy had moved to California and had fallen in with a particular group of Scientologists. Ew. He always complained about being poor. "I want to be rich," Jordy would say sometimes. Their

reply was always "Don't say I want to be rich, say *I will* be rich . . ." They said it so much that Jordy started believing that shit. Jordy decided to go to the horse races. He cleaned out his modest savings to put himself in the rich mindset: a fur coat, expensive perfume, and enough money for booze so he would have the courage to cry or break something if he lost. He got to the horse races and read the horses' names from left to right on the racing program—WE WILL PREVAIL—and a light-bulb exploded in his head. He won a shit ton of money and had it all delivered to him in one dollar bills so he could roll around naked in it. He called his mother back home in the Midwest. "The crowd I run with sure are some creepy fucks, Mama . . . but I think they're on to something . . ."

TOUR DIARIES: SEATTLE

I was in this band I used to be in and the tour stopped in Seattle. Wild times. Sorta. Last time we came to Seattle, I ended up going home with these two gay rugby players and we had the mildest time ever. So weak. I wanted to even up the score this time. This cute young boy came up to me after the show. "I like your band. You're my favorite," he says and we proceed to make out. So far, so good. I reach in his pants and find out that this boy is a bit peculiar. Or whatever. "I have a pussy" he says. "Is that going to be a problem?" "No," I say. I had admittedly never had tranny-slut sex but refused to back down because, like, what the fuck? I was already here. Why the fuck not? Not necessarily my cup of tea but by god I'll take a sip. I like the T-Boys and who could resist? All sitting around all day shooting up testosterone, getting all horny and violent like teenagers. So cute! I took him back to his jeep and started eating his ass and fucking him and he was all like, "CUMINMYASSCUM-INMYASSCUMINMYASSCUM . . ." (etc.). Damn teenagers. They sit around watching bareback porn all day thinking that cocks just shoot cum at the ready. Didn't he know I was a burnout and my shit takes longer? Either way, that annoying thing happened where we both forgot to turn off our cell phones and my bandmates kept calling and his girlfriend kept calling and it was kind of a bummer. I related this story to my bandmates when we went to Dick's Burger later that night and kept the story PG-13. I could've taken that extra step and talked about which hole I stuck it in, but honestly, I was too drunk to remember.

TRUE LOVE

1. I wanted an affair with another writer. Mr. Diaz had struck again. There was excitement in my pen and in my dick and I wasn't going to contain either. He had broken down my defenses one night outside a bar in San Francisco. I was young and wanted him to fuck me. He said, "I've read your underground magazine. You have a spark." He had a boyfriend inside the club and I (at the time) had no idea that he too spilled his guts on paper. In my (unfortunate) youthful sassiness I thought *Whatever, dude with a boyfriend*, and wondered if he had a big dick. A couple of years later in New York, Mr. Diaz, one of his girlfriends, and I walked hella far to a train, down a street, and into a cramped apartment where we all shared a bed. We didn't fuck in front of his girlfriend. Instead, when she went to the bathroom, he kissed me behind a door in the dark apartment and I could tell he was smiling. We both

went away to write. I spent more time in the underground and Mr. Diaz joined the professionals. The next time I saw Mr. Diaz he was a right grown man, with a right grown business. I wrote a fiction piece about having an affair with Mr. Diaz, ass-up and him fucking me on his desk in his office of the school he just got a fellowship to. I didn't want to be his wife. I wanted to be his beatnik mistress. I asked him earnestly, "When are we going to have a torrid affair that's worth writing about?" (I meant it.) "Isn't that what we're doing now?!" (He said that only to shut me up.) At one point, I was writing what was supposed to be the Great American Fag Experimental Best Seller. It was a twenty-six-page novella dripping with truth (and a couple of complete lies).

I nervously ask him to edit it and am secretly turned on by the thought of him telling me what to do. "Like this . . ." he says, but of course he'd never say that, he'd probably just tell me to keep going. I think Mr. Diaz is a nerd. He walks around in dweeb glasses and little "fuck me" cardigans. One day he made me nibble on his unwashed foreskin and then he gently laid me on my stomach, but of course this didn't happen. This was fiction. I didn't even know if he had foreskin, and if he did he was certainly the type to keep it clean. My foreskin stays dirty from fucking all the time, and on my third day of not showering that shit smells like three-day-old boiled shrimp water. This is a difference between me and Mr. Diaz. Upon realizing my error, I cleaned up the passage in the story to read: "One day he made me nibble on the foreskin he may or may not have. It tasted like Irish Spring." It's easy to paint Mr. Diaz in stories 'cause he's a mystery. I think of him often. In fiction, my desire motivates his goals, assertions, and actions, and I suspect if this dynamic some- how magically left the page and entered my real life, it might actually tear me apart, but I like the idea. I wanna get fucked-up. I wrote about Mr. Diaz so much I wondered if his ears were ringing. I wondered if Mr. Diaz still often thought about me. I wondered if he ever wrote about me.

2. I was a fucking nerd and I was fucking another nerd, comic book geek. We had a fetish for vintage eighties X-Men comics (back when Storm had a mohawk). I asked earnestly if he'd dress up like my favorite X-Men team leader and fuck me. I don't remember him saying yes, but sometime later, after a Tuesday night of binge drinking and pill popping, I showed up at his door at 5:00 a.m. and he answered it dressed like Cyclops from the X-Men. Then we boned. I wanted to make him my boyfriend,

but figured I should for once in my life leave well enough alone.

3. I had a little roommate who was the punk girl time had forgotten. Too punk to exist. Had a deep bro accent like Spicoli from *Fast Times at Ridgemont High*. I heard a queer knock on my door and her little bro voice, "Um, so, like, hey, man, um, Ilostmysnake, and um, if you see her, will you like grab her, andalso, I lost my scorpion too, will you grab that little guy too? Later bro! See ya in the pit!!!!" *Are you fucking kidding me? Scorpion?!?!?!?* I thought about the absurdness of dying in a dusty-ass warehouse in Oakland of a scorpion bite, but then really examined it. My other options were dying of old age, complications of HIV, or boredom. The scorpion bite would make me a legend. WORK BITCH. I immediately loved my roommate from there on out.

4. I only love boys who are drug dealers and he followed in the tradition. He grew hella pot and we fucked in his pristinely white grow room. He busted a fat load in my ass and all around us his babies were just maturing, turning into delicious dank nugs of, well, pot. I walked out of his place (with a free eighth of pot no less) into the afternoon California sun, vain as fuck, screaming, "ALL HAIL ME."

ENTREPRENEURSHIP
OR
THE RECIPE FOR LEMONADE

Turns out I had level one syphilis — *again*. So annoying, like who the fuck gets syphilis? I felt like a late 1800s London prostitute or perhaps a Roman Emperor. Either way, I got the shot with this shit injected in me that feels like it's the consistency of cream cheese. And yes, I had chlamydia and gonorrhea too. I hate those gonorrhea pills and the subsequent shitting out of the brains that follows after taking them. They asked me if I wanted a "partner pack" to take some pills for my surely infected "partner," and I said yes because I didn't want to seem like I didn't have anybody. That's when I got the idea to start saying yes to the partner pack all the time and sell the extra gonorrhea pills for five dollars a pop to all the irresponsible barebackers at the bathhouse. (I knew them all — wink wink.) By the end of the month I had made twenty dollars, and that, sir, is how you turn lemons into lemonade.

WRITING EXERCISES*

(*It was a take home writing exercise . . . "Write a poem about sex. GO!" Hmmmm, OKAY!)

SONGS FOR BOYS LIKE ME

All the boys are in love with me
'Cause what I give is free free free
No complications
Expectations
I'll let you prey on my good looks
In the back of train stations
and other dark and private places
"Oh, yeah?" he says. Well, fuck yeah . . .
'Cause son, I feel sorry for you.
You're cursed with fake boyfriends who
    demean you
He let those other guys cum right through
    his door
(The space behind his heart)

Where every other guy in town has already
    left a mess
Shitting
Eating
Not quite full enough
Crowding his plate with more
I stepped out of the enchantment
Of the buffet line
And the spell was broken
And I looked at my own plate
Piled stupid fucking high with food
And thought,
Wait, I'm not really this hungry
and also
Thank god I have a buffet now. I remember when I
    really was hungry.
The writer in the park
Read right through me
You should try being the pretty girl on a date
I try and muster the energy
To give a fuck
Fail
And think,
100 lovers stand behind me
And behind them 100 more for each
We're all taking blue pills now
Simply because
We all give way
To someone

(Some
To anyone)
For cheap.
I have dealt in Black Magic and character
    assassination
To men who thought they loved me
And lived up to only half the reputation
The confused trick spoke:
"I'm good at redeeming whores. Do you need
    some salvation?"
Ew. No.

DEEP WITCHCRAFT:
HOUSE OF PROMETHEUS

I was a member of the House of Prometheus and I can explain what that means. I had been taking normal college classes. Theater major. I had fallen in with a peculiar crowd. Something like a fraternity organization but very secretive. They called themselves the House of Dionysus, after the Greek god of drama. They were a part of a system of Houses on the campus that dedicated themselves to affiliation with the ancient Olympic Pantheon. Four times a year all the houses would meet. It was kinda predictable. House of Hades was all Dungeons and Dragons post–Trench Coat Mafia types, of course. There was House of Athena and Diana (i.e., dykes) and House of Zeus (assholes with bright futures). We were House of Dionysus. We met, did rituals, shot the shit, and had drunken orgies. Those orgies got uncomfortable. (Someone got pregnant!) About that time, me and another member decided to move on because pregnancy bummed us out. We could start doing steroids and pledge House of Adonis, but that seemed like a commitment. We thought of a different house. One we could create. We read in our Greek Lit class *Prometheus Bound*, and the legend of the fallen Titan Prometheus and how he became a friend to man: stealing fire from Zeus, giving it to the experimental race known as man, bringing on the birth of knowledge. We swore contempt against the House of Zeus (this mostly played out as *Animal House*–style pranks on those smug motherfuckers). The Head Council refused to recognize us as a house. The nature of our fallen father made it blasphemous to have open worship of him which we felt furthered our cause even more. We had to go on, meeting only in secret. We were all artists dealing in many mediums at once, but with a unifying goal and style — our work usually being referred to as "raw," "unpolished," "unrelenting," and "unfuck-withable." Our color was red (i.e., fire) and at the group altar sat a rock and a set of broken shackles.

MORE BATHHOUSE DIARIES

I was back to old habits with new tricks (so to speak). I had been crawling around the bathhouse for years and was feeling rather depressed about it, like maybe I should try meeting guys at museums or the grocery store. My friend who was sixty was over my bellyaching. "One day you'll be an old man and it's not going to work anymore, you're going to want to have a vast library of memories for when that time comes . . . every old man wishes he had had more sex than he did," he said. With that advice, I felt like someone had restamped my passport to paradise. I had it down to a science. I only went Monday through Thursday 3:00 p.m. to 10:00 p.m. This way I could catch the after work and after dinner crowd, honest gents as they were. (The weekends and anything later than ten was too tweeker-y for me.) There were still plenty of old trappings here. I was near thirty now, and still saw the same men at the bathhouse I had been having sex with here (and only here) since my early twenties. There were men I had been having casual sex with here longer than all my relationships (or whatever you would call them) put together. On rare occasions I saw these men in public, and was either shocked or horrified to see what they wore in public. Seriously. It was sometimes like, *Ew, I fucked a dude who wears sandals and cargo shorts in public*, the selfsame dude who saw me and was like, "Ew, I fucked a dude who wears daisy dukes in public." Whatever. I began to respect the fact that in the confines of a bathhouse, wearing only a towel made everyone equal (in this one way that is). Now there were of course problems. Sometimes you could fuck three hot dudes in a row. That was a good afternoon. But sometimes it was like every lonely, random, fugly dude all there at once. Like, if you put every dude shopping at Target on any given day in towels and put them in this sex maze. But then there were also jackpot days.

Tuesday. 7:00 p.m. You got there at 3:00 p.m. and since then you have fucked your way through six nationalities, six different dick sizes, and six different body types, and even took an hour-long nap with the dude who just wanted to cuddle. God bless America. Give me convenience or give me death.

There are your regulars. Andre. Twenty-three. Pilipino. You and him go to the same college. He's been positive since last year and you keep begging him to go on meds and to get the warts on his dick taken care of. You stop having sex with him 'cause you feel like it's adding to the problem. There is Mike. Forty-three. Brazilian. Though slightly taller and slightly lighter, he still looks remarkably like a cousin of yours. You and him have a similar body type. God bless Africa. He comes here every day after work because his husband of a dozen or so years won't fuck him. "Why do you stay with him then?" you ask. "Because I love him," he says. You're baffled. Like, who wouldn't fuck Mike every day? He's a babe! You have been having sex with him for years. He always has some other dude's cum in his ass while you're fucking him. It's charming and if you ever see Mike you wouldn't ask why. Terry. Terry's your big black Bathhouse Daddy. You've been having sex with him for seven years. You've been having sex with Terry longer than all the men you've dated combined. This fact blows your mind one day when you're getting fucked by Terry. Terry's a big black archetypal Mandingo-looking moth-erfucker. Six foot three. Midfifties. All muscle. He's a vocal teacher and despite having a foot-ball player body he has the voice of a church aunt. "Is that pussy cllllllllllllllllllllllllllllll-lean?" he purrs. And yes. Your pussy is clean.

Next Tuesday afternoon. Three-way. You saw both of them come in. One was Jay. Thirty-two-year-old Puerto Rican and Chinese. He dresses like a b-boy. Then Angel. Twenty-five. Moved from Mexico five years ago. Total hipster. Has a full sleeve of star outlines inked on his right arm. Deep accent. He looks like a cherub. Hairless body. Thick and well-toned. He's five foot four. He's the one you love more. During the three way, he kisses the other boy and doesn't kiss you. He doesn't use a condom with the other boy and uses one with you. You say to him later in the shower that that hurt your feelings and he laughs it off, but really you're not joking. There's a chalkboard in the back—a message board of sorts. "Room 221—Looking for Big Black Cock" or "Room 330—Regular top for ANY Asian bottom." You pause. Like, when the fuck does a top have to look for a bottom *here*? Weird. You take the chalk and scribble your room number and message, "Room 125—SEEKING LONG-TERM RELATIONSHIP," and laugh your ass all the way to your room, until, surprise surprise—there's a knock on the door. *What the fuck?*

THE BALLAD OF MR.

We had a writing exercise in Barebackers Anonymous: Who was the first gay man you knew
to die of AIDS? I had one man in mind — Mr.

Mr. was also my first memory of *any* gay
man, let alone gay and black (that is alongside
Hollywood from *Mannequin* and Lamar Latrell
from *Revenge of the Nerds*; who are both today
latter-day saints of mine but I digress). So Mr.,
this is what I remember about Mr. . . . He was
my aunt's brother in law. He owned a Camaro.
He had a Jheri-curl mullet. There were years of
my life that I "forgot" about Mr. but I tended
to remember that, as a boy, when I pictured
myself as a man, I always saw myself with a
Jheri-curl mullet. (*Ah-ha! It all makes sense now!*)
He walked with a cane and he owned peacocks. I was a little boy when this happened
and I thought that I had dreamed the birds
up, but when I called my mother and asked

about Mr., she confirmed, "Oh, yeah! He had big beautiful peacocks!" Peacocks! What a fagette!!! I feel like the late eighties boasted a very different generation of gay men. *Muthafuckin' peacocks, dude*. I'm so "modern" (i.e., emotionally checked out) that I don't even want to own plants. My father had other stories about Mr. Turns out at some point Mr. was a janitor at the local Historically Black University (the same one my parents met at and the same one I would be laughed out of years later for being too punk and too gay). My dad said he would see Mr. trolling the showers in the gym and the head had him kicked out because of it. Seeing the very obvious hole in this story, I was all like, "Well, Dad, if he was in there 'all' the time that means he was probably consistently hooking up with people . . ." and my dad was like, "Well no, son, I never really thought about it like that . . ." Years later, when my dad sees Mr. again, shit fuck Jesus Mary—he's a preacher! (He's marrying my aunt's next-door neighbor and her husband—Mr.'s brother!) I have these short snapshots in my head of Mr., but nothing that runs too long. But I only remember him in sunglasses and I remember him as handsome. Some years later (in the early nineties), I notice that I hadn't seen Mr. in years. "Hey mama . . . what happened to Mr.?" "He was gay, he died of AIDS." One sentence. These days though when I ask about him both my parents want to talk for an hour. My father gives me his version of an apology and often says of the past "Well, son, we didn't really know better . . ."

NEWEST DANCES: FLOOR WORK

I was not just an American Waiter bored at work. I was also an experimental choreographer. ("What do you mean by 'experimental'?" asked a coworker. "It means I can do whatever the fuck I feel like," I said.) I was really having too much fun with all of it. I was taking a class from this beautiful California cuckoo. He says we are going to engage in a "movement laboratory" and explains that we're also going to explore textures. "First," he said, "move across the floor as if your body is only made of muscle, then move your body across the floor as if it were only made of skeleton, then as if only tendon. On top of that, initiate movement from a place you don't usually initiate from, be it your head, elbow, shoulder, or hip . . ." At his command, a room of about forty-five dancers go across the floor looking like the zombies from the Michael Jackson "Thriller" video. There are younger men in the class. They actu-

ally move like dancers. Even in simple movement exercises they choreograph densely and
move very lyrically (I tend to move more per-
cussively). They move as if they don't have to
think very hard about it. And goddamn, their
bodies! Jesus. Their bodies. They look like they
grew up in California eating organic food and
had parents that took them to swim class —
their feet have bold arches. I look like I grew
up avoiding every moment of gym class — and
I have flat feet. This is truth. Their firmness
reminds me of my cellulite. Like, is a dude
supposed to have this much cellulite? I even
say it in a sentence in an effort to actualize and
not disassociate: "I have a debilitating amount
of cellulite . . ."

I also don't choreograph densely. My last
staged (or rather "site specific") piece was in a
DIY movie theater. An audience member came
up after she witnessed it and said, "I thought
this was supposed to be a dance performance,
all you did was walk across the theater chairs
and dive on the floor! That's not dancing!!!!!"
(said with a tone that could only be registered
as horrified disgust).

"It's a political statement . . ." I said very
matter-of-factly, just to be a bitch, and left it at
that. I don't dwell on the other boys though.
Dance class isn't about difference. It's about
commonality. We move on. The next thing is

a contact improv jam. It's all really uncomfortable. We do this thing called "base pairing" where one partner gets on all fours and the other partner planks over them belly to lower back and does a full 360-degree turn over their body. Me and my partner look at each other hesitantly. I didn't want Ms. Ching's vagina on my forehead. We barely knew each other! Pretty soon class is over and I'm washed over with the same feeling I always get at the end of dancing. That peculiar mixed feeling of running on fumes and dancing despite the fact that I have flat feet.

TOUR DIARIES: DENVER

This band I used to be in was in Denver for its second (or third?) time, and nobody had told me that it was the Mile-High City and the air was extra thin. It was the second (or third?) time I was exhausted, crashed out, wasted on the gnarly carpet rug in the basement of the Longneck, Bottle Neck, or Empty Bottle, or whatever the fuck the club was called wondering why I felt so fucking wrecked. "You're five thousand feet above sea level. That's why! You were shaking it pretty hard up there. Fuck man, you can dance." I was basically somewhat of a hype man. Got too wasted too often and shook it in my tighty-whiteys. It really was too much fun. My ultimate goal was to kill off that wide-eyed "people just standing there" era of indie rock that I felt had gone on long enough. Let's get wasted and dance and fuck. Let's get wasted and *anything*. Anything but just stand there, right?

We spend the night at a mini-squat. The fag we are staying with is kinda everything. This little Latino twinkie with glasses. I'm light-weight smitten. He has quite possibly the sec-ond-biggest dick I've ever seen on a tour, ever. I sit on it. It makes me feel good. I am of course too drunk, and after we fuck I end up stepping on a broken beer bottle in his room and go out-side in my underwear to bleed. My bandmates are outside smoking, and I go to the sidewalk to walk around in circles and talk to myself (my favorite pastime). My bandmates often comment on this pastime. They're usually like, "Dude, what the fuck?" (I'm often irritated by how easily these bitches get all shell-shocked. How the fuck are they so well adjusted? Are they on pills?) They seem genuinely dis-turbed, and I guess I can't always blame them. I really am a lot sometimes. I'm often drunk, naked, crying, blacked out, disoriented, con-fused, walking the streets of strange cities in my underwear sparking up conversations with homeless people, waking up with my hands in the pants of roadies, sucking dick in the tour van (after I was asked not to), etc. Being in a band is like being in a multiple rela-tionship with hella people at once. It really is its own unique kind of hell. We are a diverse group but, of course, diversity is bullshit. We like diversity as long as someone acts close to what we're used to. The second that's out the window, fingers get pointed, and walls start going up. I honestly feel pathologized by my bandmates sometimes. Looking back, I have to say it's very hard to discern what a truly rational or irrational reaction is when one is under a truly *absurd* amount of stimuli. I remember when the conversations became repetitive and scripted:

Accusing party: You were DRUNK!
Me: So were you . . .
Accusing party: Yeah?! Well you were DRUNKER!
Me: LAY OFF ME BITCH, I WAS MOLESTED! (cue uncontrollable crying)

It happens so much it gets to be boring. I never let any of my ego get too beat up by any disciplinary talking to 'cause alongside my admitted problem-childness I watched each of them pull what (at least I felt like) could be construed as some pretty evil shit too. You stay around anybody long enough and you're most certainly going to watch them pull some evil shit. If they don't, then that just means they're good at hiding it and that's the motherfucker you've got to be extra careful of. Either way, you're afraid to ask why you were generally the most blacked out in the band. There are of course theories . . .

And besides, bands are not supposed to revel in differences but, rather, revel in commonality. When we were on, *it* was on. I liked that. I remember that. But then time passes. You get less (or more) mad or happy about this or that. There are other sounds you're hearing in your head now.

Then there was the realization that I actually lived in a small place. I didn't want people to get to see me in such raw states on stage then be able to bark orders at me at a shitty diner. Fuck that. But despite all the bullshit, I was just glad I got to have fun, fun being sometimes so rare in life. But, it was this particular night in Denver, with my party boy wreckedness and my bloody foot, that I make a particular vow (while my bandmates thought I was simply talking to myself): "I'm not crazy," I said, "I'm writing my book."

TRIO IN SOUTHERN GOTHIC

I skipped work at the diner that day but not writing class. The theme of the lecture that day was the Southern Gothic writers. What constituted Southern Gothic genre writing, the handout explained:

> Southern Gothic is a subgenre of Gothic fiction unique to American literature that takes place exclusively in the American South. It resembles its parent genre in that it relies on supernatural, ironic, or unusual events to guide the plot. It is unlike its parent genre in that it uses these tools not solely for the sake of suspense, but to explore social issues and reveal the cultural character of the American South. The Southern Gothic style is one that employs the use of macabre, ironic events to examine the values of the American South. Racial tension and gun violence are often featured.

I took this to mean "fucked up stories about growing up in the Deep South," and, oh bitch, I got a million of them. With that much preparation, I decided to rip this genre a new asshole and wrote "Trio in Southern Gothic" . . .

1. The Graduation: I had been away from Alabama so long my family started calling me "California Boy." I had been away so long I forgot things. I didn't eat fried catfish every Sunday anymore, and I forgot about the heat or rather how it was not the heat but the humidity. But dear god—how could you forget? I also regretted things like how I never did acid as a teen. I sat on my mom's porch the night I flew in watching all the fireflies thinking, "This would look *so* much cooler if I was on acid." There was the stench of the poison the planes sprayed on the cotton field surrounding my house. Defoliant. It was used to make the leaves fall off the cotton faster, but sometimes I felt like they were secretly spraying it to kill us. The man across the street who was my mom's age and had been a farmer and mixed around with it too much had died from too much getting in his bloodstream. I had come home for the graduation. My younger sister and all the kids from her age group that had grown up in "the field"—about twenty-something kids—were going to finally walk across

the stage. I would be a witness. I took a mid-day walk because in the backwoods all you can do is walk, walk, walk, say hi to a cousin or faux-cousin (i.e., you had grown up so close and they were black too, so you're basi-cally "cousins"), and then walk some more. I looked around and cotton was not king any-more. They'd farmed it too long and it drained all the nitrogen out of the soil. Soybeans (as it was explained to me) put nitrogen back into the soil, so they grew mostly soybeans now. Up the road three houses and one crop field over was where I got attacked. I stared at the house . . .

When I was twelve, two girl cousins (eleven and thirteen) invited me over. They put me on the floor, fully clothed, one laid on my pelvis and one sat on my face and they both dry humped me furiously for thirty minutes. I remember being able to smell the younger one's pussy through her leggings and wish-ing I was somewhere else, and no, not because I'm a fag who hates pussy but because *fuck*, no foreplay?!?!?! Couldn't we have kissed with tongue first? Those bitches were jocks. Another time, I roller-skated over to the two cousins' house and four more neighborhood girls knocked me off my skates, held me down, undressed me, and all started laughing at my penis.

Years later, when I told my mother, she surmised that, surely, this was why I was gay. "Naw girl, calm down," I said. As a gay man in touch with and in control of his emotions (at least up to 20 percent of the time), I knew that my faggotry was pretty fucking epic. It seemed like a lot to blame any one person for. I kept it chill. I attended the community fish fry that was being held for the graduating babies and one of the cousins was there. She had seen a picture online of me dancing naked on a stage in Paris and said "Damn, you moved to California and got turned out, didntya?" It took quite the restraint not to slap her and say "Bitch, you started it . . ."

2. Moonshine Is a Hell of a Drug
    a. I love alcohol more than any other drug. It's the only one that calls me back and I always come . . . crawling. This, at times, leads to complications. As a child, my grandfather was a drunk and a bad ass. He'd pee in the living room sometimes and talk shit to Highway Patrol. I remember chopping wood with him and four of my boy cousins and two of my uncles one winter day. We're loading the wood in the truck and Granddad (wasted as fuck) says, "He [me] has his coat on *like a faggot!*" I couldn't have been more

than six, and I stand there all called the fuck out, and his words punch me in the stomach and I literally can't breathe. My uncle comes to the defense: "At least he's helping, Dad." I hated him for years after that—until I grew up, that is, and was ready to admit that that drunk bitch was totally on to something. I grew up to be a total doo-doo chaser. And how! He was right about the alcohol too. I left home a sober, straight-edge teen, and within a year was drinking every night and fucking anything that would fuck me back.

I came back on Xmas for the family Christmas party. It got cut short the year before when a couple of my cousins tried to shoot and kill my sister's boyfriend. That shit got squashed though, and this time love was in the air. My uncle showed up with a milk jug full of moonshine. Sour mash whiskey, goddammit. My father used to make it and told me a morbid story once. Supposedly, country men distilled the liquid through old car radiators and one chemist hadn't cleaned out all the antifreeze from one and ended up killing ten of his classmates. I had never tried it before, and the thought of dying instantly excited me. Bottoms up. Seven shots later I realized the mistake

I had made. The last thing I remember was doing the "Cupid Shuffle" with my cousins for what seemed like two hours. Blackout.

My mom (and my cousin's pregnant girlfriend) try to take me to Waffle House so I can eat and sober up, but I'm still acting a black-ass fool and get the cops called on us. We dash in my cousin's girlfriend's car to get away, but the police catch up to us on the highway off-ramp. My cousin's girlfriend is about to shit a brick 'cause there's an unregistered gun in the glove compartment. I don't remember any of this, but my mom says by the time the officer clacked on the window I turned into the perfect fucking gentleman. After they let us go, I end up giving my mom full disclosure about my entire sexual history (like bathhouse stuff and sex with my HIV-positive partner forty years my senior). The next day when I'm all hungover and alcohol poisoned she asks (very cool), "Baby, why do you think people don't use condoms? Hormones?" I shrug my shoulders and thanked fucking god I was black. Otherwise she would have noticed me blushing.

b. I learned that many people thought that my stepdad was molesting me growing up. I guess the rule is if you're a boy who is too effeminate, clearly someone is punking you out. He was a Marine and had seen the better part of the world by his late twenties. His worldliness may have made him read as an outsider to the rural community I grew up in. I later felt sorry for my Marine-butch stepdad; all he knew was that I was effeminate, read too many books, and made him uncomfortable. He mostly avoided me. What he didn't know (nor did most people) was that my uncle's friend was molesting me.

My granddad was a farmer. He grew tomatoes, squash, corn, marigolds, and marijuana. Behind my grandparents' house was this sort of field-garden that he shared with his brother and his family who lived on the other side, with a tiny dirt trail connecting the two properties. The boy who molested me (a full nine to ten years my senior—he was fifteen) would walk by me when I was alone on the trail (or sometimes when I'd pass him on the main gravel road) and would pull his hard dick out and shake it at me. I had horny older cousins and had already been exposed to porn so I knew what I was expected to do. I remember blowing him as a little boy and thinking, *Are all dicks this big??* I spent the next couple of years sucking his dick on the side of houses, by the well, and on the far side of my granddad's '57 Chevy truck. One day I told him I didn't want to suck his big smelly dick and he told me if I didn't he'd tell everyone I was gay. People by then were already calling me a fag and I knew this would seal the deal. And with that empty and retarded threat, I stayed in his servitude. He eventually started having sex with older women in the neighborhood and left me alone. I forgot about it in my teens. I even danced at his wedding with the woman rumored to be my grandfather's mistress.

I was in my midtwenties sucking dick in the back patio of the Eagle in SF. I remember the dick hitting my tonsils and the guy rubbing my ear as he asked, "How'd you get so good at that?" And I realized, *Holy shit, I've been sucking dick for, like, twenty years.* Very triggered, I swallowed.

It was another Christmas in Alabama with the family, and I got into my grand-dad's moonshine. We rode by the old house where the boy who molested me used to live in and I, drunk as a Kennedy, got out of the car, threw rocks at his house and crouched down on the ground crying. We go back to Grandma's house for dinner, and the guy who molested me shows up with my uncle. I'm still emotional and all together done with it. I took another shot of moonshine and decided to forgive him.

3. The Hunting Trip: It all started with an exercise in writing class (it always starts with an exercise in writing class). I pulled a torn sheetlet out of the hat alongside the others in my class with instructions that read: "Write about your father." I'm immediately like, *How the fuck is this a ten-minute writing exercise?* Then I went to it.

My dad in too few words: He was raised forty-five minutes outside of Selma during the sixties and early seventies. Thirteen kids and he was the younger of the two boys in the clan. Selma was a hot bed of political activity, and his small rural community, Lamison, had caught some of the run-off. His older sisters took birth-control pills and road trips to the West Coast. His older brother played in bands in Selma, and one of his sisters went to study in Lebanon (she left right as the bombs were dropping). He'd get drunk (or "just buzzed son," as he'd say) and we would go riding down the back roads. We'd listen to "All Along the Watchtower" ten times in a row, and he also loved Fleetwood Mac. As he explained, R & B radio was an urban phenomenon and didn't hit rural Alabama well into the late seventies. Mostly the older black generation (like my grandfather's age and up) listened to country music. Fleetwood Mac was the first thing they played on the country radio that had a bit of swing to it, and he'd play "Dreams" and explain that the song was how he felt about my mother.

He was a hunter. He killed a rattlesnake once to eat the meat and left its carcass on the bathroom floor, head smashed, nerves still going (I didn't know snakes could still wiggle around for hours despite being dead). I could still hear its rattles. I was taking a shit, and was convinced that my dad was a Conjure and out to get me. Other times, I would step over dead deer left in the hall so the dogs outside wouldn't get first crack at the meat. Later in life, I would come to respect a man who could kill a deer and live off of it for the winter, but as a faggy teen that didn't eat red meat, I thought of my dad as a wild man. Why couldn't we just go to the fucking grocery store? I remember he took me deep in the woods one day, pulled out a gun, and said I couldn't leave until I took the gun apart, put it back together, and then fired it just like he had showed me a hundred times before. I hated guns. I started to do it, but then I froze up, started crying, and then refused in the overarching archetypal "son stands up to father in the woods" kinda way. My father said, "What are you gonna do when some redneck breaks into your house and rapes your wife? You gonna fucking cry then too?!" The latent homosexual in me gave a terrible pause: *Wait a minute, my wife?!!?!*

THE BROTHERS OFF THE BLOCK

1. We started fucking 'cause we lived close, and also, because men with power are always an aphrodisiac to young boys. Mexican Daddy. Hella racist, and conservative to all hell. "You don't see me driving around wearing fucking prayer beads with the Virgin Guadalupe spray-painted on my car! And you *blacks* for that matter . . ." All I could think about was how I totally wanted to fuck a dude who wears prayer beads and has a Virgin Guadalupe spray-painted on his car. Well, goddamn. How come dudes like that never hit on me? Instead I get this, this (fat dicked) Brown Archie Bunker motherfucker? Bummer. I guess. Six of one? Half dozen of the other? We fucked in different apartments in West Oakland he was fixing up and making more expensive, pricing out poor families and artist types. Sorta evil. The noticeable difference in viewpoint often played out in speedy, black-and-white, polar-

ized after-sex talk about politics. He'd say shit like, "The people need to work harder—I can't believe anyone would be on food stamps!" And I'd say, "We give in to the system all our fucking lives and those motherfuckers can't shell out for some rice and beans. Dude fuck that. That's weak." (I was perhaps sensitive because I was on food stamps at the time.) Keep in mind, we had this argument with his dick still in me. He rolled off the top of me. "I was a hooker when I was your age and made enough money to eat and buy my first property. You got a dick. Use it." He was always saying problematic complicated shit like that. That's the part of him I don't miss. But there were other things. We went driving around in Orinda near the Hills and I told him I wanted to live there. "No, *mijo*." (I always giggled when he called me that 'cause it sounded sweet, felt dirty.) He continued, "These people up here. They're separated from breath and movement. You're an artist and you still have fire. You should stay in the heart of the city and create." I took his advice because I didn't really have a choice, seeing as I had no money to move to the Hills. I continued to see him because I figured I couldn't ever really think of any time that some dude I was fucking didn't completely piss me off in some way or another. Why torture him over it? He said he would wife me one day but I didn't hold my breath. I knew he was never going to leave his husband, nor did I really need him to.

2. We started fucking 'cause he lived close. He was a Yemeni store owner in my neighborhood. Seemed like all the store owners in the Lower Bottoms District of West Oakland were Yemenis. I sucked this one Yemeni store owner's dick in a van he parked in a baseball field in West Oakland a few years back and — not to be all ethnic profile-y but — I knew them to be some horny fuckers. I had been going to the store for three years, and out of nowhere dude starts hitting on me. He fingers my palm a little every time he hands me change, and I eventually give him my number. He calls me at 6:00 a.m. and I meet him at his grandfather's house and we fuck. His room is full of religious posters written in a different language. After we fuck things cool down, but then all his other cousins at the store start making passes at me . . .

3. (He was a brother from off the block.) The night started off with a metal show at my house. I like metal and feeling my "inner bro." My boyfriend from up the street comes over, he's twenty-one and from someplace in China. He's a raging commie. He yells at me about

the *Communist Manifesto* sometimes, and I let him talk shit to me because he's about the most beautiful thing ever seen. "Lay down, baby I'm going to watch the bands." He does, and I leave the room wearing only gym shorts looking like I was molested by Henry Rollins circa Black Flag. (*I wish!*) This "art metal" band from Portland (of course) was playing the same note, for like, ten fucking minutes. I go to the bathroom, and this brother with dreads (who I'd seen earlier that day up the street) slips in behind me, closes the door, and puts his back to it. I'm trapped. Not too many brothers come to metal shows so I had noticed him—dreads down to his midback. Dark fucker. 11:30 p.m. dark. Almost purple? *Why you come out here dressed like that?* I thought he was going to hit me, but he ended up hitting me with his dick. He pulls out like this *cray* fucking dick, rubs some saliva on it, and fucks me doggy-style on the piss-smelling punk bathroom floor, gym shorts around my midthighs, and hands on the front of the clothes dryer. We don't exchange numbers, and I go back to my boyfriend who is passed out in my room. I figured it'd be rude to hop into bed smelling like piss with another guy's cum in my ass, so I did the morally correct thing and took a shower before I cuddled with him.

TRES FLORES

1. The only way to explain it is this particular Mr. Flores and I loved each other; we just didn't like each other very much. I wanted him to run away with me, but then came his wife. Mrs. Flores and I always looked at each other as if we knew something that the other didn't know. Mr. Flores and I were art partners. We went to LA once and Mrs. Flores came to meet us. We all sit down to tea when, out of nowhere, Mrs. Flores starts talking about the latest article she read out of a women's magazine. "The article talked about Mexican men and how they have wives and keep male lovers on the side . . ." The second she said this I very loudly, and very noticeably, choke on the mouthful of tea I would've, under any other circumstance, certainly swallowed. Mr. Flores (being noticeably better at it than I was) neither skips a beat nor bats an eyelash. He simply looks down at his teacup (demurely), sets

the cup soundlessly back on its saucer, looks his wife directly in the eye and says (as cool as any Ice Age), "That's really interesting, honey. What else did the article say?" It was the first time I thought that that particular Mr. Flores might actually be evil, and if I was fucking Evil, what did that make me?

2. I loved this Mr. Flores in particular. He was another dancer. He danced for the company of the Postmodern Dance Hero. For this particular show, the Hero read from prose for an hour straight (as impressive a feat as dancing, I think), all flash fiction and memoir, and he was illuminated by his company dancers. Stage full of dancers. Zellerbach Hall. Row fifteen. I see him from that viewpoint. One tiny dancer-man rolled across the stage naked and I was like, "He's the one . . ." We meet later outside. He was from Mexico and had been dancing a while. He also wanted to go get wasted. I like dancers who get wasted. In the course of the night we talk about art and gods and HIV a lot. He feels one way about it and I feel another way, I learn. I think he thought I should be more ashamed about it, and I was trying to explain to him that it's hard to muster the energy to give a fuck about that sort of thing all the time. We simultaneously thought that things were different than in the past (the

Pomo Dance Hero that led his company was rumored to have been positive since before the sun had planets) and that also, at any given moment, the government could take our meds away and let us all die. I think that's part of the reason we fucked that night. Let anything Armageddon-like happen in the future, at least we got one in that night. We were forward thinkers. There may not be much time left so we'd better fuck *right now*. So, we did. I showed him a dance piece I was working on and he said when I move to New York we will marry and collaborate, but he still hasn't called me back so I don't know.

3. The third Mr. Flores was easy enough to love because I didn't know shit about him. We only ever saw each other late nights on the back of the train coming from the city. The only English he knew was "You're a little bitch" and "You like to get fucked." I sucked his dick on a train platform, and one time hooked up with him in a parking lot close to our mutual stop. I remembered he grabbed one of my ass cheeks in this intensely loving way, and how come all the men who had ever pretended to love me never instinctually did it that way? It is of course the socially legit thing to long for the touch of that man that says, "You don't have to be a ho anymore because I'm gonna make

you a housewife." I, and other girls I know, all of them being naughty by nature, sometimes find solace in the hands of a man who burns your skin with a touch that lets you know why you'll forever be a ho and perhaps never a housewife. The feeling is powerful, immense, fleeting, and perhaps not for the weak of heart.

THE PROBLEM WITH COMEDY
OR
WHY I AM DEAD FUCKING SERIOUS

I was beginning to bum out my literary agent and my classmates with my AIDS jokes and apocalyptic bullshit. ("It's always so heavy. Like, *sooooo heavy*. Maybe you should just find a boyfriend and write about that . . .") Another boy in my writing class spoke up: "I know someone who died of AIDS." After admitting this hard truth, everyone in class gave him a standing ovation. *Someone*.

My classmates were as humorless as sexual abuse survivors. Either they didn't see the humor or I really was an asshole. For example, there was the short story I wrote about the gay, disgruntled stay-at-home Castro father. He's depressed that his life has become a series of routines, has a freak out, and sells all his adopted ethnic children for meth. I was reprimanded by a classmate: "Gay Fatherhood is *sacred*, asshole. I'M A GAY FATHER!" — and he, too, got a standing ovation and round of applause.

My teacher was over me too. He marked in my papers all the time and it was always the same ("blah, blah, blah . . . I have a mutha-fuckin' PhD . . . blah, blah, blah, 'transgressive literature'" — I had to go look up what "trans-gressive" meant). I thought all these gutless bitches were sheep, and felt like they were all trying to cheat me out of the radical dialogue we should all be having about the complex-ity of the human condition, or "real talk" as they call it. No, fuck this. I decided to keep my swagger. I wasn't too keen to change for the sake of people I didn't really hang out with. It's no real blow to the ego when someone who is a shitty writer (a shitty writer who is *pleased* with himself no less) thinks you're trash. It's hard to give a fuck about someone who doesn't give a fuck about you, but being empathetic, it wasn't really hard for me to understand what the fear in their hearts was about. Comedy is a very dangerous tool. It's hard to keep peo-ple aligned with the fact that humor should never negate the seriousness of what you're talking about. This is why I think most come-dians go crazy: Chappelle, Murphy, Barr, Kini-son, etc. . . . . The trick of the balance for me has always been to demonstrate that, alongside the laughter, I'm still dead fucking serious.

HEALING

I started by writing a poem about it:

"MAIDEN VOYAGE"

On a trip to the beach
I lost my glasses in the ocean and
Took the opportunity to pray
—To Poseidon, the Lorelei, Agwe, La Serene
(Or whatever sea god or monster listening)
Kissed my glasses goodbye and said
"Here's what I've seen . . ."
Blind as fuck
And finally free
I've noticed since I've lost my glasses
More people flirt with me . . .

Here's how it started:

It was simple enough. So simple. The simplest. Some referred to him as "Ken Doll" 'cause he really was that perfect and, beyond that, was the fact that he was really sweet. In a world with some many incurable shitheads, a sweet man can get what he wants. Or rather that's how it should be, but I digress. Two years earlier, I was wasted online and asked him if he wanted to cuddle. He never responded. It surprised me something terrible when he called me and asked if I wanted to ride bikes to the beach. I agreed. Very platonic. He talks about his boyfriend a lot on the ride and since he seems to be an authority (at least to me he reads "boyfriend material" like he should wear it on a T-shirt or get it tattooed on his forehead), I asked him questions about boyfriendship like, what maybe was I doing wrong? He spills his most secret method and I was like, "Oh, that's why I'm single." (I wasn't willing to do any of that shit.) So now I knew. I feel like he can tell I'm heartbroken. We're naked on the beach, or rather I am, and all the most beautiful fags are there. We go in the ocean and he says "LET'S DIVE IN THIS WAVE!" Okay handsome dude, whatever you say. The coldness of the Pacific sobers me in this way; he looks concerned, "Where are your glasses?" OH SHIT! I dive to look but, of course, they are long gone. The fact that *he* has to point out that they're missing sobers me up too in this way, and I love what a total fuckup I am. Beyond the static of lowliness and a million failed romances, I look past the horizon line where the ocean and sky blur. A blue million miles. I take stock. There was the sun, the ocean, this pretty man, and a million more pretty men on the beach. There was friendship and also the realization that I would probably be single the rest of my life. And it was okay, maybe even preferable. And with that little bit I was healed from my two-and-a-half-year depression (if only for that day, which was good enough for me—I had felt so bad so long). I didn't worry anymore about what I didn't have.

NATAL CHART

My evil therapist had won. Again. I was coming down off a two-week drinking binge and needed something to whine about, so I scheduled an appointment with my therapist even though that bitch is my worst enemy. I bitched for two hours straight (with vigor) about being thirty, single, with no hope of fitting in and finding a stable mate in sight. "Everybody I date eventually wants to hit me," I explained. She told me I had to start putting myself in the "boyfriend mindset." My assignment was to go to Ikea (with my imaginary boyfriend, mind you) and start picking out pieces of cheap (yet *cute*) Euro-bullshit to decorate our imaginary apartment. I got high, naturally, and was so carried away that before I knew it I was in the parking lot of Ikea with seven-hundred-dollars' worth of shit I didn't need and no way to get it back to my imaginary apartment because I didn't have an imaginary car.

I could've kicked my imaginary boyfriend's ass for not taking control of me and the situation. I felt like my therapist had done this on purpose to humiliate me, and it was time to admit that therapy wasn't working. I had been going to therapy for years and I was still a raging sex addict and a creep. What the fuck was the point? Just as I was about to finally admit that maybe the problem was me, I had another idea: I figured I had a better crack at internal healing if I just paid five dollars and mapped out my natal chart, underlined my negative qualities, and either ignored them or worked on them, so I did. I entered in my information (date of birth, time of birth, location of birth) July 2, 1982, 6:11 p.m., Athens, Alabama . . .

(Things to consider: A Square creates tension between the two planets or points involved. A Trine is when two planets are 120 degrees from each other and are approximately four signs apart. A Conjunction is when it's two planets that are in the same sign. Opposition is when a planet is in an opposite sign from another planet's sign. Sextile is when two planets are complimentary, but not the same element.)

Sun in Cancer
He has a strong survival instinct and a reputation for moodiness. He is sensitive and

impressionable. He is easily influenced and sometimes manipulative.

Ascendant: Sagittarius
He has grand schemes and big promises, and a willingness to explore. He may be restless and constantly looking for something just out of grasp. He has incredible insights that may be lacking in details. He has an opinion about everything, even when feeling down he still finds humor in life.

Sun in the 8th House
He often goes further and deeper than most. He has a magnetic quality and is attracted to the taboo areas of life.

Square: Sun-Mars
In youth, he could be described as a "bundle of energy" and "can't sit still." He meets-up with his fair share of conflict, but does not fear it. He might be hot-headed and temperamental at times. His parents tried to "tame" his excess energy in youth. He meets challenges head on.

Square: Sun-Saturn
He was thwarted from self-expression in the earlier half of life. He feels unlucky at times. Attempts at control might be frequent. He may

not always see that he is his own worst enemy. When he expresses egotism in any form some part of him feels guilty. He may possess a sarcastic sense of humor, and an ability to apply caution and strategy.

Moon in Sagittarius
He needs personal space and freedom. It's hard to stay angry at him. He possesses blind faith. He is generally on the go. He prefers to "wing it." He takes great risks in throwing himself into the unknown. Bold and rebellious, he may risk everything to achieve his goal.

Moon in the 1st House
He is very sensitive and fantasizes often. He is fearful, shy, and emotional. He must learn to develop an awareness of others' feelings even if they are not as overt and immediate.

Opposition: Moon-Venus
He may give in to others too easily. He may become friends and lovers with people too readily out of a need for approval and a hunger for affection. He gets involved before considering if he actually likes the person. He sometimes replaces love with food or shopping. He can be intensely sexually active and lustful. He may possess a lazy streak.

Conjunction: Moon-Uranus
His life is out of the ordinary. He has knowledge of the world not through reading, but through experience. He likes to be surrounded by artists.

Mercury in Gemini
He is quick witted. He may come across scattered. He gets bored easily. He has a certain nervous energy.

Mercury in the 7th House
He likes to write. He comes alive verbally with one-on-one conversation.

Opposition: Mercury-Neptune
He makes errors of judgment. He lets things happen. He sometimes retreats to a dream world. He may become a drug taker.

Square: Mercury–Mid-Heaven
He is very sexually active. He has a full sex life.

Venus in Gemini
He will try to win over the object of his affection with witty conversation. He may be fickle in love affairs.

Venus in the 7th House
He tries to maintain peace in relationships to the point of bending over backwards.

Trine Venus-Mars
He is not a peaceful and calm lover

Opposition: Venus-Ascendant
He frequents doubtful company.

Mars in Libra
He is easily excitable. He often criticizes himself.

Conjunction: Mars-Saturn
He has energy and is determined. He is tough and, at times, insensitive. He is not particularly popular, but is feared and respected.

Jupiter in Scorpio
He looks for deeper meanings in things taboo or mysterious.

Jupiter in the 11th House
He achieves his objectives.

Saturn in Libra
He is not always open to new ideas.

Saturn in the 10th House
His childhood was severe. He wants to have power one step at a time.

Uranus in Sagittarius
He is shy yet bold and lively.

Uranus in the 12th House
He has a hard time adapting to new technology and the modern world.

Conjunction: Uranus-Ascendant
He is inventive.

Neptune in Sagittarius
He likes long voyages and the unknown.

Neptune in the 1st House
He will cure identity issues by taking the artistic path. He may be psychic.

Aquarius in the 3rd House
He likes the new and original. He prefers a life of change.

Scorpio in the 12th House
He wants to investigate other people's private lives.

DEEP WITCHCRAFT AND POT REVIEWS

1. I was an American Waiter bored at work. I was also a practitioner. I went to my local Wiccan priestess and asked rather earnestly "How do I fuck someone up?" (Willowy enchanted voice) "Young soul, remember the law of threes and that we must always spread peace and love and light." *Clearly* this bitch was on one, but if I walked around dressed like Stevie Nicks (circa "Gypsy") I'd probably feel all peace and love too. I was over all this West Coast woo-woo shit. The spirits crowned above my head wanted WAR. I knew I would have to honor that or face the consequences. I called my aunt back in Alabama who was a Conjure. I love all that nasty Deep South Hoodoo shit because it was *meant* to kill people. I asked my aunt rather sheepishly, "Auntie, how do I fuck someone up?" "IT'S EASY!" she said. Here's how:

a. Take an egg "straight from the chicken's duke." (I just got an organic one.)
b. Write your enemy's name on it as small as you can, followed by "run run run."
c. Go to a non-landlocked body of water and stand with your back to it.
d. Say the sacred chant:
   FUCK THAT MOTHERFUCKER
   FUCK THAT MOTHERFUCKER
   FUCK THAT MOTHERFUCKER
   FUCK THAT MOTHERFUCKER
e. Toss the egg over your left shoulder into the water.

I did all this bullshit and breathed a breath of relief. This was the *last time* Quentin Tarantino was going to assault my senses with his tawdry bullshit *ever again*.

2. My aunt back in Alabama was a Conjure. She gave me a spell that, if done correctly, would reveal the nature of the universe around me. She instructed me to sleep in white sheets, wrap my head in white, and not have sex. "NOT HAVE SEX?!?!" "Just for a day," she said, and I calmed the fuck down. I did this and dreamed . . . I dreamed of my wedding day. I looked up the stairs of the church and went with my bridesmaids to have them assist me in putting on my wedding dress. But then

like a hot poker, the voice of reason kicked in and said *Are you fucking kidding me? Dude, FUCK THIS* . . . I ran out of the church, threw my wedding dress in a dumpster, and high-tailed it for my life. I woke up and knew *exactly* what this dream meant. I called the diner and told those motherfuckers I quit. Not even a day later I got a phone call from the marijuana dispensary I had applied to; I had got the job. Twenty-two dollars an hour just to clip pot! I hung up the phone feeling like God had given me a blow job.

POT REVIEWS

Working at the pot club was the best job I had ever had. Like, *ever*. Part of my job description was reviewing pot. Some reviews:

Peppermint Kush: Sativa Power! Smokey flavor and an awesome effect! Like smoking a cup of coffee! Yum . . .

Starfruit: A good staple! I think this is a sativa I've smoked before, but I'm too fucking stoned to remember. Or care. Either way it's a smooth, piney taste that packs a punch!

Lime Kush: Smells like lime but when you

smoke it, it tastes just like pot! Just like all pot really . . . Don't trip though! Blaze this and life will get better . . . for a little while at least.

Hazy Jim: Hybrid indica and sativa and at ten dollars an eighth you can't fuck with the price. Its unfuckwithable. It smokes like a bag of seventies swag weed. Like an old feeling coming back in the night . . .

Indica: weed with a downer effect

Sativa: weed with an upper effect

FAG SCHOOL

JUVENILIA:
WRITINGS FROM FAG SCHOOL #1

CRUISING REVIEWS

1. This dude was a *sweet talker*. "You're soooooo handsome, are you a real mailman?" "No, sir," I replied, "I got these shorts at a thrift store." He wanted to take me home, fuck me, *and* buy me beer. This was way better than I did at the bar on a Saturday night, the fact that it was Tuesday morning in the park bothered me none. No cover charge, no walk of shame . . . PERFECT! I went to his house, where he had pictures of his wife and kids everywhere and every solo male jerk-off film ever. We spent three hours in the shower pissing on each other and he bought me a burrito later. PER-FECT DATE.

2. I felt a sense of mission accomplished when I finally got down in the bathroom at Gilman St. Getting it on at Gilman is problematic. Every-

one is fourteen and screwing to thrash bands takes lots of concentration. I took the easy way out and partied with a balding (i.e., post-puberty) member of the staff between bands. We kept being interrupted by a line of kids waiting for the stall so they could do drugs. I later found out the same dude wrote a detailed account of our encounter FOR HIS GIRL-FRIEND! *And then* left me out of 90 percent of the text! DIVA! Every time I'm at Gilman I scratch my head (and balls) in confusion.

3. Two hours into my friend's wedding party, I found myself in the bathroom with an older Cuban guy, *score*! "I only like you 'cause you're young and you got big lips." This was the *hot-test* thing an older dude I was blowing had ever said to me, so I got *really* hot and started going double time on his dang (he-he). He told me I had a "big load for a little gun," jizzed all over my glasses and hair and then left my drunk ass to wander the party putting on my "oh, that wasn't *me* getting slammed in the bathroom" face. (Everyone saw right through me.) And then I walked home in the rain. It was by far the hottest sex ever and I would recommend it to a friend.

4. Normally, as a rule-of-thumb-type thing, I try not to fuck dudes with Jerry beards, cops,

or men with kids because it is understood that all these things are fucking gross. I thought I'd covered the bases with this dude, but little did I know! So, I was at a party and decided to bring him to the bathroom. I kept reaching for the D and being denied. He finally explained (think: Southern accent) "I can't screw ya I got genital warts . . . LOOK!" And sure enough, he did. I had never gotten a non-erection *so fast*. He continued, "I been puttin' cream on um, but they won't go away." Some would applaud him for his honesty but, quite frankly, I hated his ass. No decent girl should have to endure this, would he pull this shit with his grandmother? He made me say things I never thought I would ("Put it away!"). And just when I thought I could be traumatized no more, "Um yeah, I should hurry up and pick up my kids, it's late." I wanted to vomit. "Oh my GAAAAWD! You're a father?! THAT'S DISGUSTING!!!!" I took the hint and left.

JUVENILIA:
WRITINGS FROM FAG SCHOOL #2

JOB REVIEWS

1. Retail: I tried to get a job at Goodwill and the lady who interviewed me was a *total dick*. She questioned my ability to be able to put like colors with like colors, and in the middle of the interview stopped and asked (very abruptly), "WHERE DO YOU EVEN SEE YOURSELF IN FIVE YEARS?" I wanted to cut that bitch, but I was crying too hard.

2. HO(stess): I got a job at a twenty-four-hour diner in the gayborhood. It was very "interesting." I worked the graveyard shift (midnight to 4:00 a.m.) and spent my nights (or mornings, rather) being harassed by drunken gay frat boys (and *believe me* that shit ain't all hot like it is in pornos) and their straight female counterparts, who because they were on hella blow thought they were so fucking *awesome*,

but who were, of course, sadly mistaken. I hate cocaine. It makes nice farm girls from Iowa do shit like move to the city, dress like hookers (the kind that don't get paid) and then roll into diners at 3:00 a.m. to have very long and unwanted conversations with under-paid restaurant hosts. Many a night I had to tell some dumb bitch to move eight feet away from me 'cause her rabbit fur coat was upset-ting my allergies. Some nights I would do shit loads of coke in the bathroom (for when coffee *just wouldn't do*), cry, and ponder my situation. *Why couldn't I just date a drug dealer?* My life would be *so much easier*. I wouldn't have to work some bullshit job at all! I do have to admit there were perks. Being sexually harassed by all the hot-bitch gay waiters was cool, and the night I worked in my underwear and made fifty extra bucks in tips was way cooler, but the *coolest* was when I got to tell that asshole gym bunny that I didn't give a *fuck* if he was Falcon Studios "Porn Star of the Year" he'd get a table when *I say* he gets a table (that shit made my five-inch dick feel twelve feet long). I wanted to give a shit when I got fired, but somehow I didn't have it in me.

3. Fundraising: Going to my telemarketing job was such *bullshit*. Every morning I would wake up and pray for the courage to turn

tricks. Being rejected by seven hundred different people *every day* started to fuck with my
self-esteem. I started walking with a slouch
and drooling (*a lot!*) I became a generally
sketchy individual, and none of my friends
would hang out with me. And no wonder! I
was hanging out with vampires! One time
this asshole sitting next to me started brag-
ging about how he upsold to a sixty-year-old
cancer patient. I was disgusted, but immediately followed suit. Soon, without so much as
a blink, I could sell to busy mothers, people at
work, people eating dinner, and even people
with no legs. Some might wonder how I got
so soulless so fast, but with a script in front
of you it's a fucking breeze. Little things got
me by at this job, like reminding myself that at
least I wasn't a child molester and, better still,
at least I didn't work retail. And there was the
time the 375-pound guy who was *always* in the
breakroom and only ate canned meat and who
fucked with everybody, fell down the stairs and
everyone in the office laughed their asses off.
The day I got fired, me and my roommate got
stoned and hung out in the breakroom for two
hours.

4. Coffee flop: I applied for a job at the coffee
house and it was *fucked up*. I sit down to the
interview with the manager, and the first thing

I notice is a big-ass butterfly tattoo . . . on her face. NOT COOL. Admittedly, I've done too much nasty shit to judge anyone for anything ever, but I took one look at that fucking tattoo and knew this shit was gonna be *so dumb*. (And I was right!) "Hi!" she said. "My name is some hippie bullshit. How are you? Okay, so the pay here is *so shitty*, and the hours are sooooooo long, and you'll be starting at the bottom, so of course, WE'RE GONNA FUCK WITH YOU. But whatever! We're all total *buds* here and hang out all the time! Do you like to hang out?" I didn't know how to tell this "free spirit" that I actually have cool friends and, outside the context of this bullshit job, I wouldn't talk to her loser trustafarian ass *ever*. But seeing as how I was hungry and needed money for weed, I decided to play it cool: "Oh my GAWD! TOTALLY! I LOOOOOOVE hanging out!" She continued: "I think the staff would love working with you. You seem so quiet!" (I could tell she meant "weak.") "We *need* more people like you on the team! I'll *definitely* give you a call!" Thank fucking god she didn't.

5. Towel boy: I wasn't getting laid very much, so I got a job at the local bathhouse. At the interview, the boss told me he dug the way my jeans fit and asked me if I had problems with

my father. He also told me that as long as I kept making eye contact with the customers I'd be everyone's' favorite "towel boy." That horny old fucker wasn't whistling Dixie; within a week I was boning down with twinks, tweekers, foreign businessmen, and my fifty-one-year-old coworker whose dick was so big I was convinced that I loved him. I also learned a lot about bathhouses, like how most of them were closed down in the early eighties, but as long as you had a sauna, you can license it as a "men's only health club." I worked with this horny Christian boy who told his preacher dad that he worked at a "men's crisis center." He explained, "Well, men gotta get off, and until they do they're in crisis, so I work in a crisis center." This was totally shocking to me. A Christian in denial? Never! But this little bitch seemed to be moving *mountains* with the power of his. I didn't have the heart to tell him he worked in a tweeker fuck pit. After working there awhile, the smell of butthole (which I once found refreshing and invigorating) made me want to *kill*. Not to mention all the mandatory work bullshit. Once a month, I attended work meetings where I learned how to more effectively mop up jizz and how to properly dispose of crack pipes. In the couple of months I worked there I only found one.

6. Food critic: I got paid two-hundred dollars to taste test snack cakes. If I had a baby I would've *sold* that motherfucker to get this job. (Sorry Jr.—you ASSHOLE!) After each "market research" meeting, I would walk a block away, light a joint, and be in unison with the universe. This shit was 100 times *cooler* (by *far*) than world peace, getting my cherry popped, or the first time I got high.

CRUISING REVIEWS

1. One time I had a really hot roommate who did tons of coke. One night, for like the forty-eighth time *ever*, I was in his room getting fucked up and helping him look for drugs he'd lost. Three shots of tequila later, as if by magic, we were slapping dicks. He turns on straight porn and asks if he can call me Brenda, his favorite girl in the porno. At this point I was too far along in the process. FUCK IT. Why not try it once? "Um, sure dude, whatever . . ." Then he tried to fuck me without a condom. "Listen baby, I don't have AIDS, I only have sex with girls blah, blah, blah . . ." *Yeah, keep talking genius.* No condom?!?! EW! If he had been my steady monogamous boyfriend or Damon (from the British pop band Blur) this scene could have been more "nego-

tiable." But this fucking cokehead? Awwwww, hell naw. He wasn't gonna get me pregnant! The thought of a cauliflower farm growing in my ass (as well as a super-powered *STD dragon* that would live in my ass and harass me at night) came to mind, 'cause I was high probably, and I was moved to *action*. "Put on a condom, YOU FUCKING HIPPIE!" He did, immediately lost his erection, and passed out. This was *quite* some bullshit. Boning down with cokehead straight dudes is *counter-revolutionary* and he didn't even have the decency to give me free drugs (that MOTHERFUCKER). I eased the tension by cumming *really quickly*, wiping my cum on one of his clean pair of socks, and leaving.

2. I was hanging out *so hard* on Polk St. I was eating fried chicken, pounding a thirty-two, and feeling generally good about life when I was accosted by this sleazy yuppie. He totally looked like my driver's ed teacher. He asked me what I was into and if I needed a ride and I said yeah 'cause I came to the city to see a show and all my friends had left and I (sorta) really wanted to suck his dick. I hopped into his blue Camaro feeling like the horny little gay boy who gets killed. And eaten. He started going the wrong way on the freeway and I DEFINITELY KNEW I WAS DEAD, but

it turned out he just took the wrong entrance and we turned around. The whole time he kept talking about some huge interview he had for manager at Taco Bell or Sizzler or some shit. I took him back to my warehouse and I almost barfed when he said, "You know it's really interesting to see how the artists and/or counterculturists of the area live." Three kids were already passed out in my room, so I tried to fuck him on a mat in a hall where we kept the bikes. Two of my roommates who lived in a tent downstairs were on hella speed and "accidently" walked in on us twelve times. He got totally sketched out, ate my cum, and left.

3. The oldest dude I ever got down with (for free) was sixty-four years old (when I was twenty). I was on the train wearing a white hanky (i.e., "dude, let's just jack off") and he was wearing some hanky that meant that he wanted to be beat up or fisted or whatever the fuck those dirty old men are always getting into. I was so happy he noticed me (I was just wearing the hanky 'cause it matched my outfit!) If someone wanted to "shake hands" with me just 'cause I was wearing a snot rag I felt it best to take the opportunity. So I did. We said our intros and got off at the next stop to find a bathroom. We get to the bathroom stall and my hanky won 'cause me beating up (or

fisting) an old guy in a public restroom would have looked weird. We finished and parted ways and the people at the restaurant all got this really confused look on their faces when we walked out.

4. I slammed three Long Island iced teas at the bar and felt like *God*. There was only one place this party was going: the video booths! I paid at the counter and went in the back. There were two Asian businessmen rolling their eyes at me and one crazy tweeked-out hairy, hippie wild man who kept shaking his hard dick at me. USUAL SCENE. Then I was commanded by a DL brother hanging out in the corner, "Get yo' fat ass in that booth!" I was happy to oblige. He asked me if I "dressed up" and I told him that I wore ties to job interviews and shit like that, but I think he meant high heels. Like this closeted motherfucker would have even talked to me if I had showed up in a wig and pumps. I'm so sure! I came and left. Some minutes later, I happened upon a teenager who had to hurry to his job at Fed-Ex (or maybe he was just wearing a Fed-Ex hoodie?) "I'm already lubed . . . let's go!" He was *so cool*. It was unfortunate when I slipped out of him accidently and fucked his taint filthy for about fifteen minutes. It was the hottest unintentional dry humping I ever had. Then I met

"Stumpy," he was five foot three, 230 pounds, and had a two-inch dick rock hard. I paid fifteen dollars to fuck him and by the time he was done with me I was a little bummed I didn't have money to tip. That shit was *sweet*. As I (finally) left the booths, I was rather proud of myself. I used condoms, and I supported trade in the community. My fifteen dollars had gone to a good cause . . . or so I thought. As I walked to my *bike*, I saw Stumpy (that *little fucker*) ease off in a brand new Dodge pickup with leather interior. I felt confused (how was he reaching the pedal?) and a little snowed.

5. I was on the train and this hella old black preacher dude made a pass at me. I'm talking long leather coat (with fox trim!), a big-ass piece of some black art home furnishing bullshit, and a big-ass Bible! Gross! Needless to say, I found him kinda cute, but I felt awfully weird about playing with his (really thick) dick as long as I did. He wrote his number on the back of one of his church programs and tried to get me to follow him to the jack-off booths, but I declined because I had to go to school.

JUVENILIA:
ROMANTIC FOLLIES

1. I saw the bullshit he usually left the bar with and I was surprised he was hitting on me. Alcohol. He was cute though, and I let him talk me up until I missed my curfew train to Oakland. He said we could make out at his house. On the way out the door, we chanced to meet the bullshit he usually left the bar with, some random Larry. That type of pale, skinny temp or yarn store worker SF was crawling with. I was sure my drunken Romeo had slept with most of them. I had been introduced to the other boy before, and I waited for that awkward moment when I get reintroduced to some random fucking white boy I didn't remember. The bitch even had the nerve to cop an attitude because I didn't remember her. *Whatever*, lady. If we were flavors of ice cream, he'd be vanilla and I'd be the most popular limited edition, okay? A one-eyed bartender friend once gave me advice to live by: "If they didn't

charm you, fuck you, or give you a black eye, then they didn't give you much to remember." I was on his team with that one.

I wasn't a boy anymore, and I saw where this was going. They started to only make eye contact with each other and started to only talk to each other too as we hopped into the cab together. It was too late to wake up friends, so I decided to wait it out at his house. My mind flashed forward to me lying awake in some strange room having to hear two strangers slurp on each other. I would have wished for a hot three-way, but both of them pissed me off. I wouldn't have fucked either of them with an enemy's dick. When we got to his apartment, the inevitable happened. I wasn't having it. I took control of the situation and left the room to make out with his roommate.

2. Love was finding me in all the most desperate and wrong places. I stood over my bathroom mirror, steam rising from the sink, frantically washing the shit stains out of my favorite T-shirt wondering *what* was the name of that big dick stranger in my room? He said he liked me, but I gave him the gnarliest case of poop dick ever, and I know I had ruined all chances of us ever being boyfriends. I needed him to leave. Love was finding me in all the most desperate and wrong places and it was

all my fault. After talking about it for five sessions with my therapist, we totally figured out where it all began; it was my first kiss. I was a really later bloomer. All my bullshit needle-dicked, acne-face skater bros had at least sucked on titties. I had nothing. I knew that being a fag was going to suck in this town. Me and my bandmate at the time went to a punk show at an old car garage that night. We were standing at the back because my bandmate was too cool to stand in the front.

I saw him dancing in the back near us, him being "Toast." Toast was a gnarly (yet somehow cute—or was I desperate?) punk rocker from California. He was thirty-five (sixteen years older than me) and looked like he had tried every drug ever offered to him. We made out in front of everybody. The next day at school these kids from a rival band told *everybody* and my queen-y science teacher told me I should be praying and "exploring safer options" in this way that made me think he was hitting on me.

3. Long story short I was fucking this way gross French dude. He had a big ol' dick and he insisted this granted him certain entitlements in our relationship. He insisted this granted him certain entitlements in life. My main problem with his "big dick philosophy"

is that it did not include very polite things. It was always "mine is bigger I top" or "mine is bigger, I'm intrinsically happier than you." It was never "mine is bigger, let's roll a joint" or "mine is bigger, I will love you forever." All this yapping about his "big dick privilege" gave me a *much-needed* complex about the size of my dick. I started having wet nightmares about the biggest dicks I had ever known: my stepfather, grade school P.E. teachers, cops, jocks, you name it! I started measuring my dick every night before I went to bed to see if it had grown any (even though I'm twenty-seven years old). I almost spent three-thousand dollars on these weird dick-growth pills, but ended up spending the money on weed instead. I gave my complicity to this bullshit because at the time it was the best I thought I could do and because he had a big dick. I had given his thang too much power and now it had power over me. FUUUUUUUCK. I wasn't going down (excuse the pun) without a fight.

I carved in stone the golden rule about dicks: size may or may not matter depending on who you are and what you're looking for; what matters *more* than that is whether or not you want to fucking *kill* who it's attached to and I wanted that French bastard *dead*.

He invited me to lunch with all his "radical fairie" friends. Radical fairies? Oh, hell no! I already know enough crazy fucking white people. He told me the guest list and I had already hooked up with most of them. I decided to stop being a hater—you have to respect the fairies because they'll usually put out. That lunch was *weak*. Everyone had fake names and hair down to their asses. They all tried to convince me to spend the money I painstakingly scammed from my parents to go hang out with them on farms, mountains, and desserts. Glue sniffers. Hell no. Frenchie made a joke about desperate bottoms and I took it personally ('cause I'm a desperate bottom). How dare he come for me and my sisters! He didn't know our pain! I took a deep breath, said a silent prayer and went to fucking war. I clanked my glass and made a toast to my beau's dick and said something about it being his only redeeming quality as a human being and they all stopped inviting me to their parties after that. I was proud of myself dodging that bullet of BULLSHIT.

I sit at my dishwashing job in Berkeley; it's at a pizzeria. I sometimes get hit on by horny, bisexual, Berkeley soccer dads. He didn't tip, and he gave me his number. "Call me," he said, "I got a big dick." I took his word for it and threw his number in the trash. Too exhausted. I'd already known enough big dicks.

4. I woke up alone to that weird pulsating butthole feeling, like when you're getting f'ed and someone pulls their dick out of your ass and there's that sort of "pop" or whatever. Anywho, I felt it waking up and did a quick finger check to see if I had shit myself. When I noticed that I was clean a *chill* of terror crawled through my spine as I looked across the empty room. I HAD TOTALLY BEEN FUCKED BY A GHOST.

5. It was Saturday morning and I was getting retardedly baked with a bunch of lady-men at the park. A very boastful friend was feeling high and mighty 'cause he was the only practicing fist-fucker amongst us. "IT'S THE MOST POWERFUL CONNECTION YOU WILL EVER FEEL WITH ANYONE. EVER" he declared, as if sharing a favorite TV show or flavor of ice cream didn't count. Really bitch? LIES!!!!

I told my side of the story. Some time ago, I was feeling grandiose and took all the shroom caps in an eighth bag and went to the bathhouse by myself. The very handsome older gentleman asked me if I was into "handballing." I told him it wasn't my cup of tea, but I'd take a sip and that I was tripping balls. He told me I'd be fine and gave me a gold star because my fingernails were freshly manicured. I took him in his room and started to punch him in the ass real good and got triggered into thinking about that old video game Mortal Kombat and the voice that comes on when you fighting partner is at his most vulnerable that yells "FINISH HIM," and I rip his guts out and hold them up in the air, mystic thunder crashing down around me. *Holy shit, man. I'm high!* It then occurred to me that I was kinda bored and would rather be getting fucked. "THE MOST POWERFUL CONNECTION" my ass. Besides his heartbeat, I felt nothing.

6. It was the summer of my seventeenth year and I was fucking *over it*. I took survey of my life and the picture wasn't so pristine. I lived in a dirty fucking house with too many other brats who, along with myself, did too many fucking drugs. I had been across the country twice on tour with punk bands where I was mostly stuck and hungry, and worst of all was my unfortunate three-way with my straight, fat, drunk, cokehead roommates. UGH! I thought of my strong, proud Mexican mother—she wouldn't put up with this shit and neither should I. Catholic guilt kicked up in my ass something fierce. I took a shower and renounced my punk rock lifestyle. I made preparations to become a Catholic priest. At first things went swimmingly. All the old ladies

at my church made me hella tasty cookies and shit. I think they were charmed by the young priesthood thing and how sexy it was. Things spiraled downward when I met that really hot priest. In retrospect, I think that romance with the priest was a bad idea. In the end, I maxed out four credit cards just so we could jerk off in religious sabbaticals in Mexico, Hawaii, and New Zealand. In the end, he admitted he had creepy intentions for the younger altar boys and I was fucking beside myself. *Make me feel old? Fuck that.* I turned that creepy old fucker in and thanked Jesus for giving me the wisdom to know I was better off in the first place. I finally gave my soul back to rock and roll and it really was a relief. I missed sucking dick.

7. It was foolish to believe he wasn't evil just because he was wearing glasses. Mistakes were made. He invited me home; on the way we had the smallest of talks. In seven minutes, I learned that he was studying art (not doing it), was an only child, a Libra, hated his father, and felt optimistic about his bullshit job. I decided I liked him. Maybe we'd be boyfriends. Long story short, he fucked me, I liked it, and two hours later he asked me to leave and avoided all my phone calls. I felt brazen and abandoned. That liar said he liked me! If I had known it was going to be that casual I

would've made him use a rubber. This scenario kept repeating in my life until I finally got some good sense and started conducting myself like a grown man. I lived by two rules. Don't give up the cookies on the first date unless you know there's not going to be a second, and if he don't want to use a rubber make him buy you a house, a ring, and a washing machine first. I saw that asshole in the park a year later and we buried all bad feelings and smoked a bowl.

BLACKOUT REVIEWS

1. It was the Halloween of my twenty-third year and I was fucking T'OH UP. I dressed as Dionysus with golden laurels and only a wreath of real grapes to cover my bits. In the end, the costume (and Maker's Mark) took control and I ended up taking on the spirit of that powerful, ancient, and wasted Greek god.

This is what I'm sorry for:

— Calling my blind date and cursing him out for ending the date early 'cause I was "kissing too many boys." They were all platonic friends that I had slept with before. Not competition. I felt so bad for bitching him out. He was a cancer patient! (When we talked later, we had an argument that led me to believe that even though he was a cancer patient he was still a douche bag.)

— I'm sorry I lost fifty dollars.
— I'm sorry for ringing all the doorbells at that Internet trick's apartment (we only hooked up once!).
— I'm sorry for falling backwards down his stairs and having the gall to spend the night. I think I hooked up with the guy that sells drugs on my front steps. If I did, I'm sorry for that too.

What I'm most sorry for:

— I guess I got naked outside the bar crying telling everyone that my father hates me and that I have AIDS. *What was I going through?* My sweet papa doesn't hate me — he's just harder to scam for money than my mom. That's all. The latter, well, that was just my paranoid drunken delusions of ill health because I was ho-ing it up. That's all. Others were not going to forgive me as easily as I forgave myself. Some positive guys got wind of this and rolled their eyes at me because they were used to me, but some positive guys (and the men who loved them) banded together in community action against me. Those motherfuckers talked shit on me like it was going out of style. They even went so far as to say that me saying

I have AIDS when I didn't was the equivalent of me wearing blackface. Even though I was guilty of it, I didn't want to be accused of AIDS-face. That's fucked up. After I apologized several times to no avail, that's when I said FUCK those unforgiving bitches. (If you don't like to see drunk people then don't hang out in bars so much.)

2. I rather unfortunately got blackout at a friend's graduation party. The next day, when I woke up at the house in a bedroom I shouldn't have been in, I got this strange feeling that my life had been ruined the night before somehow. Unfortunately, my intuition was correct. Here's what happened: Sometime in the middle of the night I stood over and pissed on this passed out boy who was a fellow partygoer. He punched me, broke my headphones, stole my skateboard, my passport, and my cellphone, burned some of the clothes I had in my bag, and I have this sneaking suspicion that he used my identity to run up an eight-hundred dollar electric bill for some random punk house in Oakland. Me and the boy shared a previous history. I drank his piss in LA one time and gave him a hummer a different time. We kissed here and there a couple of other times. He always gave me qualifiers that led me to

think everything was cool. He'd say things such as, "Hey man, thanks for the blow job." He also tenderly patted the back of my head when I drank his piss in LA. I guess me pissing on him was a deal breaker though, because he told all my friends I drugged him with marijuana and then had some teenage girl he was fucking tell everyone I was a creepy date rapist. I was heartbroken and thought for sure I'd get kicked out of the scene. But, as the story usually goes, in a month's time no one gave a shit, and six years later it's still very uncomfortable when I see him.

3. Long story short, I had basically started blacking out and walking into a friend's house and eating shit out of the refrigerator. It wasn't a big deal until my "friend" failed to inform me he didn't live there anymore. The new tenants left the door unlocked like he did. I was fucking wasted and going to town on the most delicious box of organic banana popsicles when I was tragically interrupted midslurp, "WHO THE FUCK ARE YOU MAN?" I turned around and saw these two skinny hippie motherfuckers, arms folded and looking not too friendly. They were serious. They meant business. They weren't having it. I told them I was an honored guest of my friend so and so and the shorter of the two yelled louder than the tallest, "He

moved out *EIGHT MONTHS AGO!*" He also said that I deserved an ass beating and that's when I decided I didn't like that bitch's attitude. *Clearly* this was all their fault for leaving the door unlocked. Even though I was the victim in this unfortunate circumstance, I stayed noble. I surveyed the situation and noticed that both boys were skinny hippie bitches — possibly vegan. I was just drunk enough to mop the floor with those popsicle hoarding "oh I'm gonna be free and open and leave my door unlocked and then get hella butt-hurt when someone eats my popsicle sticks" stingy hippie fuckers. If my plan went according to plan then *no one* would stand in the way of me and that box of yummy cool treats. But in that split second between thought and action a hippie bitch voice interrupted, "This is the *third* time you've done this!" I was slightly embarrassed. Who knew? I told them it was probably some other black guy, but they said it was definitely me. I (nobly) apologized, thanked them for not calling the cops on me all those other times, and left.

4. I was standing in line at the café waiting for my bagel when my recollection of the night before (which had somehow escaped me all morning) came snapping back and SHIT FUCK JESUS MARY what a doozy! Bits and

pieces came together. After the beer bust, I went to a hotel room with a very short dark Asian porn star. No sex — he just wanted to be friends. WEAK! I stole some of his underwear and left. On the train back home I looked at my balls falling out of my jogging shorts. *If I wasn't me, would I want to gay bash me?* I got off at my stop and that buff meth-head was asking me for change again. He was really feeling it and followed me all the way to the taco truck. He refused to let up, so after some shrewd negotiation I paid him two dollars to suck his dick behind a taco truck at the far end of the parking lot. His dick tasted like coffee. I started crying and called my big brother and almost pulled that whiny "WHERE IS MY LIFE GOING?" bullshit.

Luckily, he set me straight and explained his reasoning in three parts:

1. Don't trip about blowing a drug addict. There is no bigger understatement than "homelessness sucks." If you were homeless you'd want hella drugs too.
2. Not having sex with someone just because they don't have a house is discrimination. Do you really want that on your conscience? Don't be a dick! Just let it slide!

3. Besides richer parents and the hygiene thing, what makes those promiscuous, soulless, cokehead, art school fucks you scramble to fuck more "sexually credible" than the homeless guy? (I couldn't really think of anything.) Seeing it this way made me feel better, and that buff meth-head (or my lover rather) stopped asking me for change and started flirting with me more, because I guess I give good head. I was so pleased with all the positive outcomes of this scenario that I was even inspired to stop drinking for a week.

NIGHTMARE PARTY REVIEWS

1. I took leave of my senses and picked up this asshole artist. He was in town on business and had sold some huge chunk of art. I told him I'd be on the East Coast soon and would visit him in New Jersey. It all fell to hell really soon. He talked about his most talked-about work, how he dressed his mother, who had Alzheimer's, up in drag and took pictures. I certainly wasn't going to win the son of the year award but *yikes*. I let the pills and booze hit and straight-up ignored that shit. Stupid, stupid. I didn't split for practical reasons: I was horny, intoxicated, and *where the fuck was the train station anyway?* Long Branch, New Jersey, all the way back to New York—*fuck*. He started talking to me about my "writing career" and how I was doing everything wrong. I just wanted to fuck this asshole, wake up, and get a ride back to the train station. His pervy neighbor came over and I let him give me a

hand job and I think he got mad because he went all asshole middle-aged white guy on me and started letting the racial slurs *fllllly*. The train was closed till morning. This last thing I remember is getting out on the passenger side of the car, jumping on the hood, and kicking out his windshield (with him still in the driver's seat). I felt slightly sorry (at the time) and asked if we could work it out, but that's when little Mr. Asshole artist with the "outlaw" politics ran in the house (like a little bitch) and called the police. I think I still have a warrant in Jersey and that's why I don't fuck dickheads from Jersey anymore.

2. I ended up in LA at this party with a totally famous gay rapper. This fat kid kicked me out of a three-way, and then I started receiving somewhat unwanted advances from one of the rapper's friends. I guess I flirted with him a bit before and he took it really seriously. He grabbed me, refused to let go, and repeated to me in his thickest cholo accent, "Don't be fucked up." I wasn't going to fool around with him, but then relented partly because I don't know why and partly because I was mildly curious. We get to the bathroom and he wanted to fuck, but I told him he could cum on my face and that was *it*. Though I felt like I had worked hard to make the situation a mutually

loving and erotic experience for the both of us, he still told all his friends at the party that I was a stuck-up bitch.

3. It was the last time I would respond to an online ad without a picture. It was profoundly *so wrong*. The host lured me up to the Oakland Hills with the promise of shrooms. I took a pill and thought I'd be all "groovy" and get my sixties trip on with some tunic-wearing, handsome, big-dicked old white man who lived in the Hills. It wasn't like that. The host was wearing sweats and had mostly gray hair with home-done blond highlights and I mean home-done in the most fucked-up way possible. His creepy dog kept trying to give me head, and every inch of his carpet was soaking wet. He had two other boys over, Asian and white. Not to be racial, but naturally it was the entitled white boy who was the first to be over it and *thank god*. I got a ride with him and we both agreed that we just escaped some evil shit. The Asian boy didn't want to leave with us and we prayed that monster didn't cook and eat him.

4. After a whirlwind blitz of binge drinking on a Thursday night, I snapped out of it too late to realize I had ended up at a total nightmare party. Me and two of my friends walked into

some huge anonymous house. We were greeted by three twins having a three-way, snorting coke off an unopened condom box. Classic. Upstairs we met the housesitter, "Lena," who introduced herself as the world's *top* tranny porn star and showed us the cover of her latest video. Someone offered her coke and she got way pissed because she preferred speed. I felt like the night was going to get uncomfortable. She told me and my friends that we were really pretty, like girls, and that we should be taking hormones. I thought about it, and knew that if I ever decided to make "the change" that I would probably be the hottest bitch ever. But hormones were too expensive and I spent too much money on bud. I lacked the gumption it took to be a woman. I sometimes (here and there) put ads on Craigslist where I showed up wearing a wig and strategically ripped panty hose and would let straight guys hit it from the back. This was as tranny as I got, and next to Lena I felt like a total square. She started saying racist shit about black people, and it was one of those things where you're not so offended 'cause you knew it was coming. She then tried to rapport with me about how she ruined her life by getting boobs and being a porn star. I am human and was still very sore about all that racist bullshit she said, so I naturally wasn't in the mood to hear her shit. I didn't understand what she was complaining about; she had boobs and a film career. I'd seen the posters around town and knew that most people walk away from speed addiction with *nothing*. She was complaining. More uncomfortable shit happened, and it occurred to me and my drunk-ass friends that we didn't have to be there. On the way out of the door, I stole Lena's *Pac-Man* game for throwing the weakest after-party *ever*. (Some years later, photos surfaced of Lena fucking some passed-out Marine in the ass and I forgave her for everything.)

5. I bitterly lamented that the party ended up at my place. My roommate *insisted* I go get beer even though I didn't cosign on this bullshit surrounding me in the first place, not to mention my out-of-state ID clearly stated that I was underage. She kept listening to her Destroy All Monsters record *over* and *over*, and petting her cat all drugged-up creepy like (and her cat was in heat! — ewwwww!). This straight couple was smoking crack in the living room, when the woman's knight in shining armor pretends to drop the crack pipe and then pretends to load the bowl again. She's not having it (and good for her!). "Do you think I'm stupid? DO YOU THINK I'M FUCKING STUPID?!?! THERE'S NOTHING ON THERE

YOU SONOFABITCH! I BOUGHT IT!" She slams my living room door and almost breaks the glass. I sat in my room crying and puzzled. *Why oh why did I ever drop out of college? Oh, yeah, 'cause it was weak.* It later was revealed to me that even a college degree wasn't going to save me, but I continued in school 'cause, why the fuck not?

CRUISING REVIEWS

1. I took a ballet class and I was fucking horrible. My teacher was a ground-breaking eighty-year-old artist who survived multiple heart surgeries and danced in the last days of vaudeville. She told me that I had potential. She also told me to study the Mexican dancers; watch their technique. It was something about their technique. Juan introduced himself after class and I followed him to the locker room where he undid my belt, pulled down my pants, and gently turned me face first into the lockers, pulled my hips back so my ass was more exposed in the corridor of locker compartments. He rubbed saliva on his dick and tried to enter me and I told him no. He physically insisted and I didn't tell him no the second time, but I was too tense. I knew something more reasonable was going to have to happen so I sucked him off and he came in my mouth and on my chest. We cleaned up in time

before the dumb baseball players stormed the locker room. I never saw him again after that.

2. My neighborhood in two parts:
   a. It really wasn't a block for homos, but in an already crowded city I was too lazy to find another place to live. I stayed with this hot, big, black dyke who was *really feeling it* and left her Santeria altars fucking everywhere. One morning when I was too lazy to go to the bank, in an unfortunate and youthful disregard for cultural sensitivity, I took ten dollars from her altar thingy, cleaned the honey and chicken feathers off of it, and *spent* that shit. In doing so I must've pissed off one of those spirits (or *loas* or whatever) something crazy, because after that the rain came down in that neighborhood like it never had before. Getting clowned by those Korean gang members was *so embarrassing*. They made fun of my outfit! Getting mugged at knife point was *really cool*. I tried to pretend I didn't have my wallet, but my jeans were too tight and they saw through my lie. I knew it was over when I saw that *laughably large* size chunk of asphalt coming at my head in slow motion.
   b. Three years earlier, life in that part of

town had been a breeze. I lived in the warehouse district as opposed to the residential. Because of my *awesome* fucking genetics in my early twenties (to the unsuspecting eye) I looked to be in my late–early teens. This gave me choice dibs on all of the East Oakland pederasts that tried to pick me up on East 14th on my way to junior college. I recall this one day-worker, Pilipino and Mexican, in his late forties. I threw my bike in the back of his pickup and blew him off by the warehouses up the road. I can also recall walking my friend's dog and being stopped by that Goodwill truck driver. Big black dude. He looked like my uncle. His dick weighed five pounds. I was intimidated but pressed on. He wanted me to suck him off in the truck, but I didn't know what to do with the dog.

3. My mother had this totally cuckoo practice of reading all the major newspapers in California and calling me at 6:00 a.m. (8:00 a.m. her time) and relaying what all horrible things had happened in my neck of the woods. I endured years of wake-up calls detailing every arson, minor earthquake, and report of cannibalism. I didn't read the paper because the world scares the shit out of me. I begged

her not to do this. She didn't give a fuck. One morning my mother read about how everyone was catching this super-duper staph infection rash thingy, and how it was all the gay dudes' fault. She asked me if I was hanging out at these "bathhouses" and "cruising parks" and, more importantly, was I washing my hands enough? I quickly and pleasantly lied "no" and told her that her little boy was too precious to ever get fucked in a bush (LYING THROUGH MY GODDAMN TEETH). It's not that I make a habit of lying to my mother, but, fuck man, I'd lie to anybody at 6:00 a.m. just to get back to sleep. I didn't rest so easy. Much like the mother's boy that I am, my guilt for telling my mother a catastrophic lie kicked up in my ass. I dreamed I was biking to class when that invisible impact hits me from behind and slams my body into some asshole's piece-of-shit car, my (helmetless) head rolling clear across the pavement. This was my punishment for lying to my mother. My mind flashed forward to my mother flying to California for my funeral; cleaning out my dirty ass room, she'd find my sex diary. In one journal I kept a running tab of all the randoms I hooked up with at the parks and whorehouses. This way in my drunken old age I'd have my memories (of sorts), and this way I could be 100 percent honest with the people at the free clinic. My mother, though, a devout Christian, knows how to kick up her heels and have a good time. Through life, I'd seen her put that Jesus shit on the back burner if it stood in the way of her getting every gory detail of the story. She impressed me with that shit. With that I decided that if anything should ever happen to me I should just highlight the best parts of my journal. She would rather have it that way. There were, of course, kinks in the system. Like that time I was at the lake cruising and that crazy motherfucker started shaking his semi at me. He said (and I quote), "I been smoking crack and that shit makes me HELLA FREAKY. BEND THE FUCK OVER. I'M GON' BEAT THAT PUSSY UP." I wouldn't highlight him. I didn't want my mom to dwell on the fact that I fucked that guy. I would highlight, however, that other motherfucker at the bathhouse. Room 202. White dude, white (full) beard, white chest hair. He was more on the muscular side of "jolly." After he was done pummeling my crack he said (and I quote), "Son, you just got fucked by Santa Claus." I did not get a pony, but I would draw three stars by it in my journal. My mother would find this fucking hilarious.

4. Though I'm a fag, I think semen is stupid. Three seconds after climax I'm like, "Get it off of me. Get it OFF! GET IT FUCKING OFF!"

I feel all covered in bullshit like I'm on that show *Double Dare*. MY MAIN PROBLEMS WITH BOY CUM: 1. It's sticky. 2. It clumps in the shower, and 3. It smells like the inside of a dick. I went home with this creepy pagan who wanted to do this "cum ritual" whatever. We didn't even fuck! We just jerked off on each other and sat very still. SO WEAK. Was he making this shit up? I wanted to *die*, but said nothing because I also wanted to fit in though this was my own personal hell. It reminded me of this job I once had. It was described to me as "the last functioning peep show in America" where you put quarters into the slot and the screen goes up like in that Madonna "open your heart to me" video or whatever. I greeted customers, escorted the girls to and from the booths, and I was a jizz-mopper. The girls were mostly cool, moms, cokeheads, women's studies majors, and good old reliable punk girls (my favorite). All body types. One dancer wore this slutty boob shirt and matching hat that read "Harvard Medical School." I asked if she went there and she said no, but that she had always wanted to. The place was special 'cause it boasted the only strippers union in the world, but there was drama when I worked there. It was explained to me that the company became a co-op which they say dissolved the union (no need for a union if everyone is part owner), but people were still paying dues and getting ripped off. There was an article in the paper, and it was fucked up 'cause some of the girls' real names got printed in the paper. It was up in the air. I wasn't going to work there long enough for this to be a concern. I asked the head Madame if I could blow guys off in the booths if given the chance. She told me and the other fag that worked there that the official position of the company was that we could hook up with guys, but we couldn't make them cum (when they cum they stop spending money). I only hooked up with one guy and spent the majority of the time opening all the booths to that hot-boxed jizz smell hitting me in the face. I almost killed that asshole who said "you gay boys must love this job."

The Feminist Press is a nonprofit educational organization founded to amplify feminist voices. FP publishes classic and new writing from around the world, creates cutting-edge programs, and elevates silenced and marginalized voices in order to support personal transformation and social justice for all people.

See our complete list of books at
feministpress.org